Peter Remembers

AF280470

Henry Scott

Peter Remembers

The story and the people are all fiction. Any resemblance to people alive is purely accidental.

© 2005 Henry Scott
Herstellung und Verlag: Books on Demand GmbH, Norderstedt
ISBN 3-8334-2170-3

Mother was never very tall, even in heels, but I had to look up at her as she stood in the train car and reached for her furs. The two silver foxes were in the luggage rack above our seats, and she had to make little jumps to retrieve them. In accordance with the fashion of the day, mother wore one over each shoulder, their paws dangling front and back, and as she stood and looked out the window at the thin rain, the shiny glass eyes of those monsters stared down at me. By then the train was entering the Station of Baden-Baden.

Mother put on a hat, small and flat with flowers and a short veil. It was a silly hat, I thought, but at least it was black and the flowers white. I stood up beside her. We said nothing and waited for the train to stop, then we stepped down the narrow metal stairs into the wet air and began walking back toward the baggage car, a porter following close behind us.

We had ten suitcases, and these the porter loaded onto his cart, then we followed him out of the Station to the sidewalk, where we stacked them in the back of a horse-drawn carriage. We climbed in, my mother said something to the driver, and we were off toward our hotel.

The air smelled glorious, a mixture of trees, flowers, and the autumn leaves spread across the ground, all smells turned damp and thick by the rain. A brook splashed along softly outside the carriage to the left, and in the dusk I saw white bridges spanned it. Night was just arriving, and the street lamps were coming on along the avenues shiny from the rain.

Then I saw the hotel, an enormous structure blazing in light with many iron balconies, red geraniums cascading off their railings. Tall potted palms stood in front of the hotel, and I stared at them as we came nearer, for they were hard to believe, palm trees in the Black Forest.

Our carriage clattered across one final bridge to the hotel, and I realised that it was actually composed of two buildings, identical and connected by a glass roof. Uniformed porters rushed toward the carriage as we came nearer and ran alongside until it stopped. They reached for the luggage.

The main entrance was to the left. I ran alone ahead of mother and looked inside. It seemed like a palace to me, with more red, more flowers, more palms, and crystal chandeliers everywhere. Mother stood at a desk and registered, then a bellboy in a red uniform with a small pillbox hat held tight to his head by a patent-leather strap under his chin walked us to the elevator and escorted us off at the second floor.

The room was truly spacious and elegantly furnished, and I ran across it to the French windows and pushed them open. There was the balcony with the red geraniums, and down beneath was the brook, just a strip of shiny light. A large colonnade loomed across the way, but it was already too dark to see clearly. The air was sweet. I had never smelled air like that before.

From near the door at the other side of the room my mother said, „Well, this is our new home now." She looked around vaguely and added, „I hope not for too long. It must cost a fortune." Then she said, „Go wash your hands and brush your teeth. It's dinnertime."

I did as she asked and when I next looked at her eyes I saw they were shiny with tears. She took me by the hand and said, „This time we'll walk down."

And we did; we walked down that wonderful grand staircase, across the hall, and into the dining room for dinner.

This was in 1941. We were there in that wonderful room with its geraniums because of the war. It was hard to hold onto homes during the war. Our first home was an apartment in the middle of Düsseldorf, but as soon as the bombs began to fall nearby we moved to a house on he edge of the city. By the time we moved to that house I was nearly six years old.

One night I was in bed with the mumps in that house in Düsseldorf. It must have been late, and I had been asleep for a long time, when I awakened by a terrific explosion. The windows of my room came flying in toward me, and I heard only a terrible roar. Shattered glass covered everything, and thick dust and pieces of plaster fell from the ceiling onto me in my bed. I pulled the eiderdown coverlet over my head.

For a few seconds after the blast there was no sound at all, just a deathly silence like that in a mausoleum, and that frightened me more, I think, than even the explosion. Then the alarm sirens came on with their own ear-splitting sound, and I could hear my father, mother, Annie, our maid, yelling my name. I could hear the three of them running up the stairs toward my room yelling at each other and for me.

My father was first in the door. As he came in I sat up in the bed. He looked at me, looked around the room, shouted back toward the door, „He's alright," and the added, speaking only to himself, „thank God." I could hear my mother crying somewhere on the stairs. My father lifted me straight up out of the bed, swung me around onto his back, and carried me piggyback out of the room. My head was so high I hit the glass globe of a lamp hanging from the ceiling, and I shattered and fell, adding more glass to the floor.

We all rushed down the cellar, supposedly the safest place in the building, and huddled there together in our nightgowns surrounded by shelf upon shelf filled with glass jars preserving last summer's harvest from our garden. We listened to the sirens, then to the silence, and we then walked back up the stairs.

Except for the broken glass and fallen plaster, our house was not hurt. We had been truly lucky. Our neighbour's house just a few yards away across the street was badly damaged. Their son Klaus was my age and my friend. He and his family stayed with us for a few days until the debris was removed from heir house and new windows put in.

The bomb that fell in our street was the only bomb that fell on Düsseldorf that night, it was the first one dropped on that city, and it made all the papers. The story was that an English plane had been hit by anti-aircraft fire, and the pilot, before abandoning his plane, had dropped his last bomb. He was found the next morning very much alive, hanging from a tree, his parachute dangling near him in the branches. He was taken prisoner and had told someone his tale. His plane had crashed in a field. Why the alarm came too late was, of course, never mentioned in any of the accounts.

That single bomb was altogether too much for my father, and it made up his mind for him. He wanted mother and me safe and out of the industrial city. A week later she and I left Düsseldorf.

I was in a new world, one I had never seen before. The war had not scratched Baden-Baden, and life went in there as it always had. It was peaceful and beautiful, that famous spa, and I loved it. The only misfortune was that I had to leave all my toys back home in Düsseldorf and, being an only son, I had plenty of them. I missed my dolls. I had quite a family of them, including an Eskimo, given to me by father's friend Mr. Glotz, who travelled a great deal. But most of all I missed Helga, a doll my mother had given me the Christmas I was four years old. My mother often told me the story of that Christmas. There had been other toys for me, a child's desk with chair, lots of tin soldiers, and other gifts, but I had a beeline for Helga, and nothing else interested me, much to the shock of my father.

Mother and I went to the Kurhaus, Baden-Baden's municipal building. The middle is an Empire building with many columns that had been enlarged on both sides. I later found that it housed one of the most famous and beautiful gambling casinos in Europe. Besides that, there were two restaurants, a theatre, and a large open-air terrace where girls served apple juice in native costume famous for big red pom-poms sewn on straw hats. Sweet mother, always aware of my weakness for dolls, discovered a marionette theatre in the Kurhaus and promptly booked us two seats for the afternoon performance.

I had been with mother to the theatre at home. She was a great theatre fan and believed her son should experience it as young as possible. The „Merry Widow" was my first. I understood nothing of the plot, but enjoyed the dancing, the decor, and the costumes.

My second theatrical experience was not nearly so successful. It was supposed to be „Hänsel and Gretel", but for reasons unknown we found ourselves facing instead „Don Pasquale", which I found boring. Later I finally saw „Hänsel and Gretel". The director, a friend of father's, let us use his box and took us backstage during intermission. What a factory was hidden back there behind those velvet curtains! I was thrilled: this was my first sniff of grease paint.

But I had never seen a marionette theatre. We went up the broad green-carpeted staircase into the theatre. It was a normal theatre but its stage had been made, a small man in tails appeared and announced the show. He said his name was Mr. Kuno. Hanging on black strings in front of a black velvet curtain he looked quite real, hardly like a puppet at all. The show was „The Revenge of El Hakim", all in a Turkish setting and extremely exciting and gruesome since El Hakim's head was chopped off on stage and when it was later presented on a platter to the sultan, the head was still talking and cursing the monarch. All very realistic. I was ready to jump out of my seat.

Back in the hotel, I was still so excited and my face was so flushed that mother put me in bed, felt my forehead, and then took my temperature: fever. She called the hotel doctor on the phone, and he soon appeared, examined me, and gave his diagnosis: scarlet fever. Although this was by no means the height of the tourist season, the hotel was packed, all the rooms taken by people like us who had left big industrial cities to escape bombs. A boy with scarlet fever could not be permitted to stay around so many people, so mother and I again climbed into a horse-drawn carriage, and off we went to the local hospital.

All my life, I had never been separated from my mother. To have left father behind was sad, but I was a mother's boy, that was nothing to deny, and I didn't look forward to being left alone in the hospital. The hospital was run by Catholic nuns, and we were Protestants, but as everyone agreed there was a war on, and it was the only place available.

We had to say goodbyes at the door because mother was not permitted to enter the ward, so full of people with infectious diseases. I made a terrible scene, but in the end one of the nuns got a good grip on my jacket, dragged me inside and shut the door. She led me down a long corridor and into a room that was bare except on one of the beds, left the room, and I suddenly found myself alone for the first time in my life. I got into the bed, pulled up the covers, and cried myself to sleep.

A cheerful nun wearing a tall starched white hat awakened me the next morning. All the rest of her was black except for a pale crucifix dangling and glinting over her expansive bosom.

As she bustled about the room she spoke to me in the local dialect. I had become accustomed to that dialect, and she spoke it with a warm, motherly touch that had a soothing effect on me. The bed I was in was against the wall, but other beds, including one near the window, were still unoccupied, and I timidly asked her if I could move over to the window.

„Sure, sugar, no problem", she said in her sweet version of the dialect, and I found myself owner of the bed near the window. I was lying there at noon when I heard little stones hitting against the glass. I looked out to see mother standing outside in the rain in the garden, waving to me. Since she was not allowed inside and there were no telephones, she had found this way to communicate. We shouted back and forth for a while and then developed our own form of sign language.

Later in the day the doctor came by on his rounds and informed me matter-of-factly - that I would, of course, have to stay in the hospital for at least nine weeks. I was shocked. Nine weeks is a long time for anyone, but an eternity for a little boy. I was destroyed. Faithful mother came by every day, rain or shine, and brought me my favourite cartoons, „Die von Schreckenstein", a story about an ancient portrait gallery in a castle where all the paintings come alive at the stroke of midnight and then do their best to scare the living daylights out of the castle's current owners.

Having nothing better to do, I cut paper dolls out of the cartoons and glued them in an album and wrote my own stories underneath them. Sister Margret, my friendly nun, loved it and couldn't get enough of my stories.

On the fourth day not only my mother appeared in the garden but also my father. He had somehow managed the long journey in spite of the gas shortages. He'd written out a sign for me and held it up so I could read it: „By Easter you will be out." He had meant well with his sign, was trying to cheer me up, but Easter came and went, and I was still in the hospital. By then a thirteen-year-old boy also with scarlet fever had occupied the second bed.

His attitude toward the hospital stay was different. He was, in fact, quite glad to be away from his family for a while. His name was Casper, and he told me about his large family, local people and not at all well off financially. He was a nice-looking boy, but perhaps a little too loud and boisterous. Since he was so much older than I was, I believed everything he told me.

He thought my cutting out paper dolls was absolutely ludicrous. His mind was firmly fixed on other subjects, and the truth is that he could hardly wait to share his thoughts with me.

He told me that in his family's home he had to share a bedroom with his older sister and her husband. „You see, Peter, I pretend to be asleep, and when my sister and her husband come to bed I watch them making love. I'm only thirteen, but for my age I already have a big dick." He lifted his blanket to show me his erect penis. „My brother-in-law's is three times my size and thick like a bockwurst. You know something? He puts that big thing into Sis's pussy, and she doesn't mind. She moans and groans and lobes it."

I sat there in bed absolutely speechless.

Casper then took a bottle off the nightstand and tried to push his penis into it, explaining as he did so, „Pretend this bottle is my sister's pussy. Well, he puts his thing in and out and in and out until he comes. But before that he puts a rubber on to keep her from having babies. They can't afford children yet. Everyone says so."

„Casper", I asked, „what is a rubber?"

„Well, Peter", he said, „it's made out of thin rubber so that the come cannot get into her."

„You're telling me that without that thing your sister might have a baby?"

Casper threw up his hands. „God, you are naive. How do you think your parents got you? They fucked, of course."

I found this information at once fascinating and revolting, confusing but also extremely interesting. I whispered across the room to him, „You're actually saying that my mother and father did that?"

Casper laughed so hard I feared he'd bring all the nuns running.

„But, of course. That's how children are made."

At that point, sitting there on that bed, I did not believe him. It was just too grotesque to contemplate that my sweet mother would ever do something so disgusting. I stared at him in wonder.

The bottle was back on the nightstand.

„Peter, believe me, that's how it's done. You'll find out later that I'm right. And, by the way, it feels terrific. If you don't have a girl, you can do it by yourself. I mean you can get the feeling, if not quite the same."

With that he started to massage his still hard penis, first slowly, then faster and faster. His eyes closed, he groaned, and white shiny liquid sprinkled over his belly.

„Ah, you see, that felt great", he murmured.

He took a towel from the nightstand and wiped himself off. Then he pulled his shirt down and pulled the blanket up under his chin. „I'm tired", he said. „I'll take a nap."

Pebbles knocked against my window, and there was mother, standing alone in the garden. Father must have gone home. We waved and threw kisses through the window, and I thought, „Casper is a low-class idiot! Lies, nothing but lies! He's just a big show-off. My mother would never dot that. Or maybe yes?" I looked out at her smiling back at me.

I was released before Casper and never saw him again.

It was raining again the day mother came to fetch me in a closed carriage pulled by a single black horse. We walked together through the corridors and said goodbyes to all the nuns. Sister Margret gave me a big hug, squeezing my face against her crucifix and her soft chest, and asked me if she could keep my album of paper-doll stories for the amusement of other young patients. I handed it over. Outside, the coachman sat atop his carriage, looking somewhat forlorn in his raingear. Water flashed off the shining flanks of the lone horse.

Then the horse's hooves clip-clopped over the cobblestones, and I was free again. I leaned across and looked out the carriage's little window, smeared with raindrops, and saw that spring was coming. There were bright new leaves on the chestnut trees we passed, jonquils were in bloom, and golden forsythia was spread along the avenues. The lawns of the Lichtentaler Allee were a sea of yellow and mauve crocuses and again I found myself smelling that sweet air, this time mixed with the leather of our closed carriage. The rain had almost stopped, and mother held my hand.

„We don't live in the hotel anymore", she said. „They've passed a new law that allows visitors only a three-week stay. But Mr. Steiger, who owns the hotel, rented us rooms in his villa. He is forced by law to take people in, and the offer was made to your father. The villa is very large and beautiful. I'm sure you'll like it there."

We passed the rose-colour theatre with its wide flowerbeds in front, wet blue and yellow pansies sparkling in the few rays of sun. The carriage made a left turn, and the horse pulled us up a steep street.

„There it is, Peter", mother said, pointing into a park at the top of which stood a building. We drove past big iron gates, the main entrance to the estate. My mother explained that this entrance was seldom used anymore.

„The smaller entrance is on the top at the same level as the manor house", she explained. The road became more winding and steeper until we reached a smaller gate that opened onto a narrow lane lined with chestnut trees that led right to the main entrance of the house. It was enormous, as big as the hotel, but mother kept calling it a villa, a new world for me.

The villa was a famous landmark in Baden-Baden. An American had built it during the early twenties, but he had left Germany after the stock market crash and sold it to Mr. Steiger. It was a replica of a Palladian-style Italian villa and was eminently suited to its surroundings. It had a light, cheerful feeling, with many stairs, loggias, terraces, a fountain, a pergola, and lots of beautiful urns, all planted with geraniums. The view was beautiful toward Mount Mercur and Baden-Baden down below us. The villa had eighteen rooms, and father rented a dressing room, bedroom, and bath on the first floor as well as the main dining room, which was separated by a carved-wood arch from the living area. Behind this room was a large live-in kitchen and a pantry. A spiral staircase led to the upper floor. Next to the living room was a terrace with a view over the entire estate.

I was impressed, even overwhelmed, by all the beauty. I loved that place from the moment I first saw it.

No one was in the house when we arrived. Mr. Steiger was in his office in the hotel, his only daughter, Helen, was in school, and her governess was out shopping. Mr. Steiger had been divorced for many years and lived in this palace with his daughter and her governess, taking their meals in the hotel, which is what we also planned to do. I tore off my raincoat and began exploring the empty villa from top to bottom with great relish. It was the most beautiful house I had ever seen. Our house in Düsseldorf, which I had once thought so large, seemed a joke in comparison.

As I ran from room to room mother was following somewhere behind me, calling out my name. She finally caught up to me in the loggia, which connected with Mr. Steiger's living room.

„You mustn't go into these rooms", she said. „They aren't ours."

„Oh, Mother", I said, „nobody is here, and they'll never know if we take a look around."

She had not dared to look over the house, and I could see she was as curious, as I was, so together we looked at all the rooms, from the great hall, the salon, up the grand staircase and through the bedrooms, until we reached the maid's quarters. They were not being used, since hotel personal came twice a week to clean.

Once I had the layout of the house fixed in my mind, I put my raincoat back on and went outside to explore the grounds. I found a hothouse hidden from the villa by trees, and on the other side, also hidden from the main house, was a building in the Bavarian style with a big garage. In it sat a monstrous car, propped up on blocks and covered from top to bottom by a tarpaulin. I lifted one side of the tarpaulin, opened a door, and climbed into the car.

I didn't know it then, but I was sitting inside a vintage 1927 Rolls Royce. It seemed like a wonderful car to me and for a moment held all my attention with its dark wood and leather. Then I heard a strange noise, a kind of gurgling, coming from just under the roof of the garage. I got out of the car, took a look, and found a long rectangular cage filled with wonderful exotic doves, almost white but a few light brown. I learned later that raising these graceful birds was Mr. Steiger's hobby.

When I walked out of the garage I nearly collided with two people coming along the path toward me. The man was tall and slender, the woman tiny and fat.

I saw the man had kind eyes. He said, „You must be the young man from the village. We heard you just got out of the hospital, and look at you, you're already running all over. That could be dangerous, you know."

We shook hands, I told them my name and discovered that I just met Mr. and Mrs. Vernin. He was the gardener, responsible for all the flowers in the hotel and on the estate, and she was the laundress for the villa. They both liked children, not having any of their own, and Mr. Vernin and I became good friends. What I know about gardening he taught me, and with great patience.

She was very shy and did not talk much but was a perfectionist at her craft. I shall never again see linens and shirts cleaned and handled the way she did.

They lived in an apartment over the garage and asked me in for a moment. The apartment was small, spotless, a little old fashioned, but very cosy. Mrs. Vernin prepared a cup of hot chocolate with whipped cream for me, delicious and quite a treat in those wartime days.

I had forgotten my mother, and by then she was frantically searching for me. She heard our happy voices through the open windows and knocked on the door. When she entered the apartment I could see she was angry, but she had not yet met the Vernins and said nothing in front of them. They offered her chocolate, too, but she refused with the excuse that I should be in bed resting. After all, I was just home from the hospital.

„I'm sure they're very nice people, but that's no excuse for running off and leaving me sitting by myself for so long", she complained to me once we were outside alone.

„Just like your father", she said, „always running off to the blue horizon. You must rest. We don't want a relapse."

The park became a dream as spring progressed, with hundreds of blooming rhododendron bushes, all of them under the close supervision of Mr. Vernin. We knew there was a war going on, but not in Baden-Baden, not in the Black Forest.

One day as we made our way to lunch at the hotel mother asked me about the boy who had shared my room at the hospital.

„He was okay", I said, „His name was Casper."

„He was older than you, thirteen, I believe", she said.

„Yes, he was thirteen."

„Well, what did you talk about in all that time?" she asked.

She was just making conversation on our way to lunch, but I still had many things on my mind, put there by Casper.

„Mother", I blurted out, „is it really true that Dad fucked you without a rubber?"

She stopped dead in her tracks. Her face turned a bright red, it looked to me like the colour of tomatoes, she took a deep breath and then another two steps forward, and then she stopped again and turned to me.

„Don't you dare to use those words ever again! They're filthy! So that boy, that low-class boy, talked about things like that. I am shocked!"

I could see that she was, very much so.

„Mother, please", I said, „I didn't believe him, but that is what he said, and he said that is the reason why I was born. He told me."

„Oh, dear Lord, I wish your father were here", she hissed.

„Well, tell me how it all works. I want to know if he told me a lie or the truth", I said.

We walked together slowly. „We cannot talk about this in the hotel, so please do not ask me questions over the table. You must promise me that."

„Yes, Mother, but please tell me."

Poor mother. I could see she was in a quandary. She thought for a moment and then slowly, haltingly, and us-ing the best of German, she told me about the birds and the bees. By the time we reached the hotel, I knew it all. It was all the same story Casper told me, only now I knew it in High German.

Little drops of perspiration were on her forehead. She took a handkerchief out of her handbag and wiped them off before entering the hotel.

„You go ahead", she told me as we walked through the main hall. „I have to powder my nose first." She walked off, and I went into the dining room.

We always had the same table.

„So", I thought as I sat alone at the table. „He fucked her after all." One could say that mother's halo became slightly tarnished for me that day. One could say my personal age of innocence was over for good.

Very close to us sat a lady at a small table. She always wore a big straw hat. Always the same, rain or shine. Only that day she had the company of a young man. It was obviously her son. He was in uniform so we guessed he was on leave. I noticed his hands; they were the colour of a purple blue. When their lunch was served, his mother cut everything up for him and started to feed him. His hands lay immobile on the table.

„What is going on mother?" I whispered.

„Oh, that poor young man, his hands were frozen in the war." It was at this moment I realised; there was another world out there somewhere I knew nothing about.

The loudspeaker paged Mrs. Jaqulay. Mother jumped up and ran out of the restaurant, leaving me with Goosebumps. It could only be a call from Düsseldorf. „Dear God, let it not be Dad!"

It seemed like an eternity until she came back. She read my face.

„Dad is alright", she whispered.

„There has been a Blitz last night on Düsseldorf, half the

city is destroyed. A firebomb hit our house; the top floor is gone. But there was not enough water, so father and Anna tried to kill the flames with wine and champagne, can you imagine?"

I started to cry, all my toys and dolls were gone.

„Stop that immediately", she said. „There are plenty more toys in this world, you silly kid. The factory was on fire, too. Nobody helped Dad to get the fire under control, except the prisoners of war. You know the roof is tar and it was so hot it melted. Your Dad fell and started to slide and would have fallen through the big glass roof when one of the prisoners grabbed him by the legs and pulled him back. His left arm is badly burned. Your Dad could have been killed, and you cry about your silly toys."

We had finished our soup when the call came but now neither of us could eat, so we called a taxi to take us to the villa. Mother immediately put on the radio for further news, and we were in for another shock.

The speaker announced we were at war with Russia.

„It is going out of hand", mother said. „You must understand one thing, as young as you are, never, but never, discuss with anybody what is said in this house, is that quite clear?"

I was scared to death. It had been quite a day, I promised to obey and I did.

„Now father needs a rest. We are going briefly to Düsseldorf and then we all go for three weeks to the seaside before we return here. He want us to leave tomorrow, I shall go now and pack."

By then I felt instinctively that not all adults were for war, it was a lot to digest in one day but I managed. To cope with several things in one day was a lesson I never forgot.

This time we travelled with only one suitcase. The train ride was a nightmare. Army personnel first, of course. We sat in a compartment, usually for six, but now with nine people and most of the time I sat on mother's lap. The trip, usually four hours, took us eight, but we made it.

Dad was at the station, his arm in a sling. The drive from the Bahnhof to the house I shall never forget.

What once had been a lovely city lay in ruins and rubbles. Our house looked dreadful. Instead of windows, there was cardboard. The inside was a mess, because of the smoke from the top floor, the ceilings had fallen down, and dust and bits of plaster everywhere. From my former room I looked into the sky. A few strings on a wall indicated that once I had an upright piano. Poor mother was absolutely destroyed and cried most of the time.

Dad had built a bunker under the factory, so that his workers, who mostly lived in the neighbourhood, had a shelter to run to, when the alarm was given. Since that happened every night, we did not stay much in the house but mainly in the bunker, anyhow from six p.m. on. There were blankets on benches so one could stretch out, until the bunker filled up, and then we sat like in a sardine can. Some people dozed off, but most of them were awake. One night at eleven, another raid on Düsseldorf.

At that time the heavy bombs had been invented. Often four of them were coupled together, that could destroy a whole block. Except for that first night years ago, this inferno was new to mother and me. The people who had experienced these raids before became hysterical. Nobody knew if their homes would still be there once it was over. Or worse, would we be hit directly?

The bunker, all solid cement, enforced with iron beams, shook like a cardboard box. I could hear the bombs coming down. First there was a whistling sound, then a few seconds silence, until impact. One could judge approximately where they had fallen.

That night the target was the harbour on the Rhine, not

far from us. The danger was great that the factory would be hit again. The people were feverishly praying to our Lord. Babies were crying, the air you could have cut with a knife. An old man next to me shit his pants.

Finally, the all clear sounded. Slowly they packed up their belongings and left, a troop of tired, grey looking people frightened what to expect when they got home.

The factory had not been hit. The next morning very early we left.

Our destination was a seaside resort near the Danish border. We travelled in two cars. The three of us in one and Dad's partner, Uncle Joe, his wife, Aunt Ellie, and their daughter, Lisa, in the other. I called them aunt and uncle since I knew them forever but we were not related. Lisa was a few months younger than I was, and until we left Düsseldorf we had grown up practically like brother and sister. Aunt Ellie and Lisa lived in a different spa during the war. It was wonderful that we were all together again for this holiday at the sea, after all, we had not seen each other for a long time.

We stayed one night in Hamburg in a big hotel near the Alster. We saw little of the town, except Lisa and I remember our doorman who was our height but looked like an old man. His uniform was similar to the bellboys' in Baden-Baden. His voice was that of an adult and so were his manners. We were fascinated with this little man but, of course, we had never seen a Lilliputian before.

That night we had an alarm and trundled with all the other guests into the hotel's cellar. We children fell asleep. No bombs were dropped that night, it was not Hamburg's time yet, that would come later.

That year we had a glorious summer. The sea, the mighty ocean, was something new to us children. We loved the little town, our little hotel and the beach but that ocean frightened us. People were actually jumping into those waves and seemed to have great fun. And the taste of that water, God forbid! Reluctantly we out our feet into it, when our fathers grabbed us and took us piggyback into the sea. We screamed our lungs out and were sure never to see dry land again. The fathers made a great afford to calm us down while dipping our little bodies into the salty waves. It took a while for us to get used to our new environment. Once we had the hang of it, our parents could not get us out any longer.

The three weeks passed very fast. We were all tanned from head to toe; the ocean had become our friend. Those wonderful lazy days playing in the sand, while the adults sunbathed in those wicker contraptions that mushroomed along the sea.

That vacation was to be long remembered. The sea was now our friend, and would never be forgotten; alas it would take years to see the waves again. The last night there was music; we dined on the hotel's terrace. The adults danced. The men in white and our mothers in floating gowns made out of chiffon printed with flowers and puffed up sleeves, their hair rolled up over a contraption called „the rat". We children in sailor suits were allowed to stay up with the adults. The lampoons were swaying in the soft breeze and the waves crashing onto the beach. How beautiful our parents were, so happy and carefree, and so much in love!

Our return trip was uneventful.

Back in Baden-Baden I became a regular visitor to the marionette theatre, that is I became an addict.

Soon the whole staff of the Kurhaus knew me, from the box office to the ticket taker to the usher. It was always first row. I began to memorise the text of the whole repertoire of eight or nine plays. Most of the plays were fairy tales, except

„El Hakim" and an eighteen-century comedy. I did not know then that two people spoke all voices only. The male and the female voices had the ability to change so drastically that one got the impression of at least ten people speaking behind the stage.

As it happens to actors who do the same parts over and over again, one day, the lion in „Cat in Boots" got stuck in his dialogue.

Sitting in the front row, I whispered the next line. The lion recovered and finished his part.

After the performance, the usher stopped me.

„Herr Direktor Eberts would like to talk to you", I was informed. „I told him that you are here for almost every performance", he continued.

We stepped outside the theatre into the foyer. A small side door opened and out came a little man with grey curly hair, wearing thick eyeglasses, followed by a tall blond lady. Smilingly they shook my hand and asked my name.

„So, you were my souffleur today! I thank you very much, it was embarrassing there for a minute, even my wife could not help me out", he said.

I blushed; I had not expected that from Herr Direktor, as he called himself.

„Is there something I can do to show you my appreciation?" he asked me.

Of course there was something! For weeks I had been dying to go backstage to see how it all works.

„Could you please show me around backstage?" I asked.

„But with the greatest pleasure, my boy", he laughed. „Just follow us."

„Fräulein Becker", he called, „we have a visitor, my helper in need is here."

I was introduced to Fräulein Becker, an older lady, also wearing thick glasses.

„You see, Peter, Fräulein Becker is just hanging back into their proper places the figurines we worked with this afternoon.

„Please put on the lights", he told her. He then climbed two tall steps up onto a platform the length of the stage. There was a railing the same length, wide enough to rest one's arms on. This was extended on either side with small beams and hooks to hang figurines in a row as requested to their appearance on stage. Herr Direktor gripped the lion from Fräulein Becker whom she was about to put away, let him down onto the stage, and started to roar while his tiny hand manipulated the strings. The lion came to live, his tail wagged, his head rolled and he opened his fearsome mouth. Eberts winked at Fräulein Becker. She took a sheet of metal and swung it from left to right. Thunder filled the stage. She then flicked a switch and it was pitch black. Eberts lifted the lion quickly upwards, hung him on a hook behind him. The lights came on again and Mrs. Eberts, during the short blackout, had put the mouse on stage and let it run about. I was astounded. So, that's how it was done, that's how that big beast became a little mouse!

They all looked at my perplex expression and laughed.

„Now you have seen one trick of the trade", he said climbing down, „but of course,there are many more."

„I tell you what, Peter. Saturday, we'll play the „Three Wishes". If you like, you may watch us work backstage."

Would I ever, just wait until mother hears of that.

„Thank you, Herr Direktor, I shall be here!"

„Well, run along, performance at three p.m., but you can come earlier", he called after me, as I ran out.

Mother listened attentively to my new adventure. She realised I had no friends my age but hoped that would change the following month when I would have to attend school. The alphabet, she had taught me already. I could read the time and add and subtract, I was well prepared for the Adolf Hitler School. However, Saturday seemed an eternity away.

I started to fabricate my own first marionette. It was to be the snake dancer who opened the variety show after Mr. Kuno. Mother helped me buying cotton wool, yarn, needles, rests of fabric and so on.

Mr. Eberts' figurines were works of art. Carved out of wood, each one created by the artist Ivor Puhony who had died a long time ago. My dancer had to be crafted out of fabric since I did not know the art of carving. We found an old doll whose head I would use. Mother had found the doll, and I decapitated her and repainted her face, cut her hair off and replaced it with a pyramid hat cut from cardboard, glued over gold foil, sprinkled with gold glitter. It came out a mixture of Egypt, Bali and India, but that did not matter, it looked definitively oriental. Her body was fabric, stuffed with cotton. The limbs were thin branches covered with cotton and sewn into fabric. All this would be covered by a wonderful costume. The snake was still a problem but all that had to wait because Saturday was here.

At two p.m. I was backstage. They had just arrived and after a brief „Hello Peter", were busy getting ready for the show. I noticed their teamwork. Everybody knew exactly what to do. Fräulein Becker put coloured celluloid slides into the upper side stage lights made out of tin cans with strong white bulbs inside. Then her attention was given to the record player still to be cranked up. She stacked the records according to the variety acts. Mrs. Eberts hung the figurines left and right behind the wings in accordance to their appearance. Mr. Kuno first, then the snake dancer and so on. Mr. Eberts stacked the scenery and the backdrops in the order they were needed. They barely talked to each other, with such an old team instructions were superfluous.

The minute the audience entered, silence was important because also it looked like a wall from outside which separated us, it really was a gigantic frame covered with painted forest green canvas except for the stage frame, in order for the spectators to hear the dialogue. It was before microphones and all that electrical stuff used today.

Most of Fräulein Becker's activities were stage left. For reasons unknown, the strings for the curtain were stage right, so she had a lot of running to do.

„Peter", Eberts said, „when I nod to you from up here, you open the curtain or close it. Can you do that?"

„Of course, Herr Direktor, I know the repertoire by heart", I answered proudly.

„I know, that's why I will entrust you with the curtain today."

The last thing they all did was to take their shoes off and step into old soft slippers. Fräulein Becker started the intro music for the arriving audience. Mrs. Eberts looked with one eye through a peephole and counted the audience.

„Only fifteen today", she whispered to her husband.

He shrugged his shoulders. „The weather is too good."

The house lights went down slowly, the intro music stopped. Mr. Eberts put Mr. Kuno centre stage. He nodded to me, and I opened the curtain. A slight bow of Mr. Kuno to the audience.

„Ladies and gentlemen, a heartily welcome to the Baden-Baden Artist Marionette Theatre under management of Ernie and Winny Eberts. „ He then fell into his routine and finally announced the exotic snake dancer.

Then to the joy of the audience he explained that he was entirely in the hands of his master who only had to pull a string or two to remove him from stage. With that Eberts pulled him slowly up while Kuno was waving at the audience. Applause, a nod from Herr Direktor, and I closed the curtain. Becker quickly changed the lights; Eberts dropped an oriental palace painted on canvas. Winny put the dancer in position, Eberts held the main stick, and Winny took the smaller one on which the dancer's hands were attached. Becker started the music, and I very slowly opened the curtain. The stage was now in dark red. The figurine was a remarkable work of art. Painted in a café au lait colour with Siamese headdress. Bare to the waist, tiny breast, the nipples, each the head of a tiny gilded nail. She wore wide pants of gold lamé and golden slippers turned up at the toes. Over her shoulders, the snake made of many articulated copper pieces.

She was the only puppet that needed two people to manipulate. Winny manipulated her arms and hands, and Eberts the body and the snake. She always opened the show. Usually three variety acts were shown, but was a play that followed too short, one ore two more were played.

During her dance, Becker changed on her side the lights from orange green to yellow but on my side the light stayed red. She was my favourite act, I think also with the audience.

Since the theatre was created in the twenties, we also had the dolly sisters. They sang and danced to an English record, which was especially cared for because under Adolf it was impossible to replace.

The play that followed, „The Three Wishes", was a moral tale about human disbelief and stupidity. A lumberjack is working in a forest when he hears a voice inside the tree he is about to axe down. Inside the tree is a fairy begging to be released. The lumberjack opens artfully the tree and there is this beautiful fairy. Out of gratitude she grants him three wishes before she floated gracefully out of the tree.

In the second act, in his home, he tells the story his wife who does not believe him one word and thinks he had one too many. However, there is no dinner waiting for him because they are so poor. She makes him a big scene of the lack of money all the time. He is tired, hungry and confused, and she keeps nagging on. She would like so many sausages to last her all winter, and cajoles the poor man to prove that his fairy could provide them. It is all too much for him.

„Well, have your darn sausages already", he yells at her. With that a huge bowl with sausages appears on their table.

His wife is overjoyed at this miracle. He suddenly realised that he had spent one wish but his rage over his error upsets him so that he screams,

„I wish these sausages came out of your nose." One, two, three, the sausages are coming out of her nose, the bowl is empty.

Now all pandemonium breaks loose, his wife is in hysterics. Try as he may, they are permanently attached to her. He is ready to cut her nose off but she wails and pleads with him. He gives finally in and wishes them off. His three wishes are spent. The fairy enters the kitchen, enlightens the audience about disbelief and stupidity and floats off the stage, the bowl with sausages at her feet.

Even then I loved the idea that this good fairy did not even leave the sausages to these poor people behind - but that is Germany.

In a marionette theatre strings do everything.

The axe of the lumberjack was put between his hands by a rubber band but the axe had to have a string to lift his arms. The tree, a prop of course, its front was held by a string, so it could fall open. Its top had to be open, so the fairy could float out of it. The sausage bowl was light papier maché, held on four strings, so it would not turn. The sausages had two strings; one went to a tiny hook of the woman's nose, the other to get them back into the bowl. The illusion of reality had to be ever present and the Eberts were masters at it. I admired them and Fräulein Becker tremendously.

„One time we had four in help", Eberts told me. „But he is at the front now, and to find help is impossible during this war. You, of course, are very young. I know you love it all and you are so dedicated. I think, I must meet your mother. If she agrees to help us permanently, we would love to have you", he said, and continued, „it could be just a volunteer job, unfortunately we cannot pay you. Times are bad, you know we had only fifteen tickets today. Its not what it used to be anymore."

The idea of making money had never entered my mind. I was so proud and honoured to be of help and agreed on the spot, providing mother would consent.

One afternoon, the three met in a coffeehouse, I was excluded and spent the time to sew the costume for my own snake lady until mother would return.

She tried unsuccessfully to hide her pride about her sonny boy. The Eberts had played her compliments about my enthusiasm, my love for the theatre, my keen observation so forth. She gave her permission to work with them.

I kissed and hugged her; what a mother I had!

Performances were only twice a week, Saturdays and Sundays, it was a rule from the ambitious Gauleiter then, reasons unknown to me.

Twice a week I was there, if only in charge of the curtain yet. My burning desire, of course, was to be up there with them and handle the puppets.

That day came when Fräulein Becker had the flu.

I could overhear the Eberts talk about their dilemma. Thirty tickets had been sold on that rainy day. They did not want to cancel and took a chance on me.

We played „The Three Wishes" again but it could have been

anything else, I was ready, but Frau Direktor was uneasy.

„He's only a child, only seven years old", she told him.

„Don't worry, my dear, that boy will not disappoint you." Eberts said. „He has already copied the snake dancer in his own fashion. He shall bring it by, and you can judge for yourself."

Early that Saturday morning, the Eberts sat in the audience to watch my work of art on their stage.

I was backstage in frenzy. Lights were set, record ready, backdrop down, and my puppet in position.

The stings on my dancer were not long enough, so the Eberts would see the bar and my hands, but that did not matter. The puppet on the hook, mid stage, the record on and then I raced to open the curtain, climbing quickly on a crate so I reached the balustrade and the dance could begin.

I had no help, so my puppet's hands hang loosely on rubber bands, giving the illusion they would move, anyhow, her arms were lifted high enough, what I thought was an oriental position.

My snake was an old necklace of mother's black onyx pearls, which she reluctantly had handed over to me.

With my one hand, the snake rose slowly while my other hand changed the lights to green and gold. The dance continued just as the Eberts' puppet. Then mine had to make an exit because I had to close the curtain. Applause from the Eberts who came running backstage.

Winny took me in her arms and gave me a big kiss. A demonstration I had not expected from that otherwise cool lady.

„Truly lovely", she cried out, „now you are really one of us."

Mr. Eberts beamed, „Good show, my boy. Now let's go on with the three o'clock performance."

The show ran as if there had never been a Fräulein Becker in the house. Winny was flushed and perspiring afterwards but ever so happy. It was always so hot backstage, and she usually worked in her slip. But quickly she had her dress on and a big hat and took my hand.

„Ernie, you will find Peter and me on the grand terrace downstairs. We shall have the biggest ice cream they can make", she shouted over her shoulder, dragging me out of the theatre downstairs.

From then on, I was one of them, which turned into a long friendship that lasted until they died.

Finally, my first school day arrived.

With a leather bag, stripped on my shoulders, which held a small blackboard, a crayon and a sandwich, it felt heavy and uncomfortable. Was that to be the first burden of life, well it would be.

In my arms I held a „Tüte", it looked like a clown's hat turned upside down, filled with sweets. Was this a warning to sweeten up front for things to come? It certainly was.

I wore short pants, short socks, that thing on my back and the paper cone filled with sweets. Mother, of course, in a dark blue, tailored suit, me in hand, off we went to the Adolf Hitler School. Nazi flags were flying; the director of the school made a long speech. Then we all sang „Deutschland, Deutschland über alles".

„Behave yourself in class", mother said, „this is an important day in your life", and left me with the other kids to scramble into our classroom.

We were thirty children in one room, two to one desk. I found myself in the third row from the teacher's desk, which was raised on a dais. My neighbour, called Norman, was also an out-of-towner in Baden-Baden for the same reason. His home was not far from Düsseldorf, I found out. After looking around at that noisy bunch, I soon found out they were all locals. We were the foreigners.

Everybody spoke local dialect, except Norman who still could not imitate their accent.

Into all that noise entered the teacher.

Poor old thing, had been pensioned off at sixty and was now sixty-five to teach the bunch of us. He definitely was not ready for his new task. He carried a long bamboo stick in his hand, which he banged on his desk until the class fell silent.

I did not pay attention to all this gibberish but designed in my head my second puppet, which had to be Mr. Kuno, of course.

Norman had the same way home that is to the hotel, where I met mother for lunch. We did not talk very much. He was as boring as class had been.

„Tell me all that happened today", mother wanted to know eagerly while I looked at the menu. Potage Crème Helen, again, which I knew by then meant a potato soup.

„Our teacher is over sixty-five. He told us something how we had to behave because of the war and what wonderful soldiers he would make of us, that is, if he lives that long."

„Now, don't be flipped", she said.

„Mother, it was all very boring", I replied. „You know, mother, I thought the next puppet should be Mr. Kuno. I have him almost ready in my head, details and all, but please, you must give me a hand with the tailcoat."

Mr. Steiger entered the dining room and came to our table with his professional smile on his ugly face.

He kissed mother's hand, „Gnädige Frau."

„Peter, I hear this was a great day for you, now you are a pupil in the Adolf Hitler School", he addressed me.

I thanked him, getting up bowing, as mother had instructed me.

„This afternoon in the villa, I would like to have tea with you, gnädige Frau, and your son. My daughter Helen will also be there. Now you are both in school, is that not nice?"

He bowed towards mother and disappeared.

I had never liked this slimy man with his tiny forehead and the little hair that was left pomaded down in the middle. His daughter, Helen, however, was a beautiful girl with chestnut hair and big blue eyes. When she smiled she had the cutest dimples in her cheek. She was always very busy with her school. Two years older than I, and always protected by her governess, Miss Urner.

Mother had befriended Miss Urner, and sometimes they spent evenings together knitting and chatting.

Every chance I had, I would corner Helen. Seldom did we have time to walk in the park and talk but we liked each other a lot. She had no hobbies and lived my stories about the theatre. Her German essays left a lot to be desired and occasionally I helped her, mostly stories about the marionettes. Miss Urner, of course, got wise to the whole thing but did not mind giving a hand to Helen.

„It's the first time Mr. Steiger has invited us, Peter, and all because of your first school day. That is really very sweet of him, don't you think?" she asked. „All you can dream about is your next puppet, you better pay attention in school."

„Mother, please, the teacher only gabbed about our Third Reich."

She quickly changed the subject. The potato soup was served.

Mr. Steiger's „tea" took place in the grand salon of the villa. Besides him, Helen, and Miss Urner, he had invited his architect and wife, Mr. and Mrs. Lakers. He was a bore but not she. Her hair was white which became her very well because of her fresh complexion. She was full of fun, pedalling with her feet the automatic machine pushed in front of the Steinway Grand. Everyone was for „Carmen". It was a performance in the municipal building at that time. She found in a stand nearby a white roll, put it into the machine and started pumping the two pedals with her feet. The grand piano sprang into life after a few of her pumpings and there was Carmen. She fancied herself as a singer, and while the piano played the Habanera, she sang - sotto voce - along with the music. Her husband was a very handsome man. Probably her age, with a little grey moustache, which was not the fashion then and seemed reserved for Adolf. Their only son, a lieutenant, was at the front.

The adults, I noticed exchanged amused glances with each other when Mrs. Lakers was off key, which she was lot of the time but they indulged in her fund. Helen and I looked at each other, She was bored as I was, and we sneaked out of the salon.

„Do you want to go upstairs?" she asked. I nodded.

We climbed the spiral staircase all the way to the top. Helen had a room there, not her bedroom, just a large room filled with toys. Everything was very much in order and all things looked brand new to me. It resembled more a toyshop than anything else.

„These were all my toys when I was little", she said.

„But Helen, they all look so new", I said.

„Well, I never had other children to play with and by myself it was just no fun. You can play with anything you like, even when I'm not here."

Her generosity touched me, and I told her that all my toys had been destroyed at home.

„Oh, just take whatever you want downstairs", she told me.

„What is in this big wardrobe?" I pointed to a large piece of furniture with a mirror in the middle.

„Oh, that belongs to my father", she said, „I think it is locked."

I tried one door and then another and they were not locked. Curiously we looked inside. In the bottom were rows of ladies' shoes, on the racks were dresses, cots, capes, and on the top shelf, hats. Again, it all seemed hi good condition. The smell of mothballs filed the room.

„My God!" Helen cried, „that was Grandmother's wardrobe."

„Would it not be fun to try some on?" I asked.

„Oh, let's have a laugh."

We costumed ourselves to show off downstairs.

„We shall be two elegant ladies."

Helen put on a light blue velvet gown, which suited her beautiful auburn hair. She found matching shoes, a little too large, but we put paper inside to make them fit. Then came an enormous round hat decorated with birds, flowers and ostrich plumes in a pinkish colour. Over all that, we found a black velvet cape trimmed in ermine, a little yellow by then. She looked quite the grand dame. I chose white lace and a turban hat with a bunch of Egret feathers sticking up in the air. White satin shoes and a long white fox stole.

„Seeing our reflections in the mirror!" we screamed.

Carefully, we manipulated the spiral staircase to the second floor and went down the grand staircase arm in arm.

„I tell you what, let's enter the salon just chatting but not looking at anyone, and then sit on the large sofa and ask for a cup of tea", I instructed her.

Mrs. Lakers was pumping Viennese Waltz while we descended. Since the sliding doors were open to the salon, they saw us coming down the stairs. A lot of Ooh's and Aah's as we grandly sailed to the sofa and asked for tea. Then the adults were all around us, and we had to parade our finery for them.

„I just can imagine whose idea that was", mother laughed. Mr. Lakers took us to the terrace to take some photos. Only Mr. Steiger was not amused which he tried to conceal without much success.

„Now that was just lovely", he said stiffly. „Now, you two, take it all back upstairs and put it neatly away."

„Yes, Papa, of course", Helen said meekly.

We did as we were told. Helen was very quiet. I sensed her father had not approved. Perhaps she should have asked his permission first. Poor Helen had to ask permission for everything. Her father was very strict.

In school, the class was to be silent when the teacher entered. Everyone on their feet, then after „Heil Hitler", we could sit down. One day I was telling Norman about Mr. Kuno who was almost ready when I missed the teacher's entrance. Norman pulled me up.

„Heil Hitler!"

We sat sown and I continued my story. Teacher looked around.

„Are you still talking?"

I stood up. „Yes Sir, I was."

„Come forward", he commanded. „Bend over the first desk."

He waved the boys at the front desk out of their seats.

„I shall teach you to talk in class only when asked", he said.

I had to bend down; he pulled my pants very tight and then hit me four times with his long bamboo stick over my rear end. I ground my teeth. It hurt terribly and that old goat, was he strong.

„Sit down", he said pointing to my seat. Sitting down hurt even more, no matter what position I tried. That day at lunch I had the hardest time concealing the story from mother.

Thank goodness, the chairs in the hotel were upholstered. I was so ashamed because I had never been hit in my life. That night when I undressed, I kept my front towards mother and tried to get into my pyjama pants as fast as possible. But I had forgotten the big mirror in back of me. It was floor length, held by two console tables for my mother's toiletries. She saw my bloody rear end in the mirror and foyer red and blue welts across it.

„Turn around", she said. „Pull your pants down."

She examined my buns.

„For Heaven's sake, Peter, how did you get that?"

My composure was at its end. I put my arms around her and started to cry bitterly.

„It was the teacher, he hit me with a stick." I cried. I then told her the story. She put me into bed on my stomach and went into the bathroom to get wet towels, cotton balls and witchhazel, and started to treat my wounds. I had never seen her so outraged. She was white as a bedsheet.

„In all my life I have never seen such cruelty", she shouted at the top of her voice. „Does that man not know that corporal punishment is outlawed? Oh, they have not heard the end of this!"

Her voice became threatening.

„Now, turn slowly around while I put a pillow under your behind", she told me. „My poor darling". She kissed me. „Does it hurt very much?"

It was a rhetorical question. Next morning she took my hand and marched with me to the Adolf Hitler School. She walked fast and did not say a word on our way. Once arrived, she made straight with me to the director's office. Brushing the secretary out of her way and dragged me into his office.

„I am Mrs. Jaqulay, this is my son Peter who is on your school in class A under Mr. Burger."

Her voice was shrill. She turned around so suddenly and before I knew she had my pants and underwear down to my knees and showing the director my naked rear end.

„This is what happened in your school, Herr Direktor. That sadist Burger did this. I shall lodge an official complaint with the police and I want that man removed."

To me she said „Now, Peter, pull your pants up."

The director was visibly shaken by this unexpected early visit. When he regained his composure, he started to plead with mother.

„Gnädige Frau, please, not the police. Please, no scandal, we are the Adolf Hitler School."

He was wringing his hands.

„I wonder what the Führer would say about how his new youngsters are treated by an old sadist", mother replied sarcastically. „Mr. Burger is old, too old for a class of thirty youngsters."

„I know, but we have no other person here, you understand?"

„That is no excuse, Herr Direktor. I will take Peter out of class for one week. I want a letter of apology from Mr. Burger, and then Peter transferred to class B with Fräulein Dump", she demanded.

„Yes, gnädige Frau, I shall see to it. I am terribly sorry", he stammered.

„Good day, Herr Direktor", mother said. She directed me out and slammed the door. I was very proud how she handled the whole affair except that she had shown my naked rear end, but I guess that is what's called evidence.

Just before Christmas 1943, father arrived with Annie. I was very fond of Annie who had been with us for years. She was a country girl when my parents engaged her, but since has been citified. I still remember she had sausage curls in her black hair but they had gone some time ago. We were all very happy to be together for the holidays. On Sundays I always went to church, sometimes with mother, often by myself. We were not particularly religious but it had always been this way since mother's mother was alive who always went with me. It was just one of those routine things to do on Sunday mornings.

That Christmas we performed a church play. I was one of the shepherds and had a few lines to speak. They all promised to come and see it. Even Dad consented. I think he had not seen the inside of a church since he married my mother.

Dad had arrived with all sorts of goodies, and we were in the kitchen baking cookies and making marzipan, which was dipped into hot chocolate as a frosting. Father made pretzels, mother rolled little balls called marzipan potatoes. Annie was busy with the dough, and after it was rolled flat, I pinched out different shapes with the help of tin forms. Dad also brought a gramophone and lots of records. Every so often, we played Christmas carols and everyone sang along. Then came the preparation for the Christmas cake. We were all busy cutting up the ingredients while Dad worked the heavy dough. Uncle Joe's parents had been bakers, so father knew a lot about baking that he picked up with Joe when they were children. Finally, he worked all the ingredients into the dough. It took him quite a time, then he tasted it. His face went ashen. He tasted it again, took the whole dough and lifted it, and threw it on the table in disgust with a big bang.

„It's ruined!" he shouted, „absolutely ruined."

We were stunned.

„Somebody gave me the wrong bag. It was salt, salt not sugar!"

He left the kitchen in a huff. Annie tried first.

„It was salt", she said.

Mother tried, I tried. It was salt all right. The dough was ruined. Two identical brown bags on the table, and Dad had used the wrong bag. Annie started to cry.

„I pushed the wrong bag towards Mr. Jaqulay."

„Annie", mother said, „don't cry, it was an easy mistake to make. Look, they are identical."

Annie ran after father into the living room. Still crying, she said, „Mr. Jaqulay, maybe if we put the dough overnight into water it might help."

„Nothing will help. Throw it into the furnace", father screeched at her.

„But, Mr. Jaqulay, we used all the ingredients, the flour, everything that is hard to come by", Annie pleaded.

„Throw it into the furnace, you dumb cow!" he screeched.

Annie came running back.

„He says..."

„Yes, we heard, Annie", Mother said. Then turning to me. „Actually, you tasted everything, the chocolate, the marzipan, the nuts, why did you not taste what was in those bags?"

Oh God, now it was my fault. Well, Christmas was jolly good, even without the fruitcake. They all saw the church play and were pleased. After church we had dinner at home. They liked the tree I had trimmed. It was my job from then on and for many years to come. Then came the gifts. For Dad I had found a second hand book about the industrial age. For Mother I made, with Helen's help, a large coffee cosy. And Annie got a hat, which belonged to Mother. But Annie didn't know that. But what a surprise when Dad opened the door and pushed a bicycle inside for me. Wow! I couldn't believe it. My own bike. Dad started to explain it to me in great detail but I could not wait until morning to try it out. So he took me to the terrace, and I curved around and around.

Annie was so happy that night. My parents had bought her a wonderful dress. I thought actually too elegant for her but there was a reason for that. Mother and Dad were going to Düsseldorf in two weeks, and Annie had to stay with me and have lunch at the hotel. First day after my parents had left; Annie was a bit nervous. She had dressed up for lunch in that dress and hat.

„Peter, what do you think?" She asked me uneasily.

Annie had never eaten in an elegant hotel.

„The shoes must go, Annie", I said. „Go up and put on Mother's black pumps, she'll never know."

Annie listened to me in matters of taste, and I wouldn't steer her wrongly.

„Annie, wait", I called. She came back. „Show me your hands."

She stretched them out. „While you're upstairs, put on a pair of white gloves of hers, the three quarter ones, you know where her things are. And put some lipstick on." She blushed a bit but did as I told her.

„Well, well", I smiled as she came downstairs. „Quite the lady. But listen, Annie, I'm sure you don't mind when I say in the hotel that you are my aunt?"

„All right", she laughed, „I'll be your Aunt Annie."

We started to giggle, looking at ourselves in the mirror.

„Okay, ready to go?" And off the hotel I went with my elegant aunt.

Annie was a movie fan, she had studied the stars of the silver screen, and I knew she would not fail me. For her, of course, it was all like a dream but one that she enjoyed a great deal. All the personnel there knew me, of course, and vice versa. Annie took my arm when we entered.

„Good morning, Peter." It was the concierge.

„Good morning, Mr. Eberhard." He glanced at Annie. „Good morning, gnädige Frau."

„Good morning", Annie answered. The same thing in the dining room. Rollie Pollie, Mr. Walter, held Annie's chair. He was our headwaiter.

„Good morning, Peter."

„Good morning, Mr. Walter, this is my Aunt Annie", I said.

„Welcome, gnädige Frau", Mr. Walter gave us the menus and bowed to Annie who smiled.

„Your Frau Mother and Mr. Jaqulay are not in Baden-Baden?" he asked.

„No, they are in Düsseldorf for two weeks. That's why my aunt is here", I answered.

„First time in Baden-Baden, gnädige Frau?" he asked Annie.

„Yes", she answered.

„Well, I hope you have a good stay." With that he left.

Annie started to relax and carefully studied her new surroundings and the clientele of course, who in turn studied her discreetly. Some noisy ones had to enquire behind their menus at Mr. Walter who she was. But Annie did not notice. My apple juice was put before me automatically.

„Aunt Annie, would you like a bottle of mineral water?" I asked before the waiter left. Annie nodded.

One look, blah blah, for Madame, he wrote down.

„What did he say?" Annie asked.

„Oh, they like to speak French. Wait until you read the menu."

In those days the menus were very simple. One soup, one main dish and one dessert. If you liked it or not. After all, it was war. Annie stared at her menu.

„I can't make that out at all", she whispered to me.

I told her the soup was potato soup. The omelette is a pancake with cut ham, and the soufflé in French is a rice pudding with strawberry sauce.

„I wish they would say so", countered Annie.

After lunch, we sat in the hall and ordered coffee.

„Why are we sitting here? Why don't we go home? I can make us coffee", Annie said.

„It's only 2 p.m., we have an hour."

„An hour for what?"

„Well, today is Saturday, and I'm helping out at the marionette theatre at 3 o'clock", I said and told her about my latest hobby.

„It will surprise you, never having seen a marionette theatre."

Suddenly she gripped my arm and sat straight up. „It's him, Peter, look, it's him!" she whispered excitedly.

Down the grand staircase came a tall handsome man in full dress ready for horseback riding. I had seen him before and knew who he was. It was Joseph Wrath in the flesh. For a moment I thought she would faint. Wrath was then the German movie idol of all women from 18 to 80 and working on a film in Baden-Baden. He took a seat in the hall almost across from us, and Annie could not take her eyes off him. His chauffeur appeared and they left. Annie was on cloud nine and dream-walked next to me across to the municipal building. I bought her a ticket and took her upstairs into the theatre where I deposited her in the first row.

„Where are you going?" she asked me, having completely forgotten my story.

„You just sit and enjoy the performance and afterwards I will pick you up", I said and rushed backstage.

„We are late today", Eberts said.

„Well, I had to take care of the maid for lunch", I said.

Eberts shook his head and Winny gave me a very strange look but it was too late to explain. Fräulein Becker cranked up the gramophone, and we started the performance.

Afterwards, Eberts said, „We have to talk to you."

„Oh, just a minute, Mr. Eberts, please." I opened the curtain and leaned onto the stage. The audience had left, but Annie still sat there.

„Meet me downstairs at the café. I'll be down there soon."

Then I said to Dieter, the usher, „Please, Dieter, show my aunt where the café is." He nodded and showed Annie out.

„So", Eberts said, „you had lunch with your maid and brought your aunt to the performance." He ran his fingers through my curly hair. „You're quite something." Then he became serious; we all sat down and listened to him.

„When Purhony died he had finished the last figurine for the fairy tale „The Princess and The Frog". Not only that, but the sets also. But it has never been performed. The figurines are exquisite, so are the sets, and Winny and I have finished the dialogue etc. There will be three acts. The fact is that technically it is rather complicated because of blackouts, quick scenery changes and so on. We would like to perform it but we would need a lot of your help including manipulating three different characters on stage."

I was thrilled. A premiere and I was included. We got permission to use the theatre every day for four weeks only. That was not much time, it would mean rehearsal every afternoon. I would stay after lunch from 2 p.m. to 5 p.m. with a regular performance of Saturday afternoon, of course. All eyes were on me now, then came the question. „Do you want to do it?"

„Yes, of course, I would love to do it." I could hear Winny and Fräulein Becker give a sigh of relief.

„However, I have to talk to your mother first to get her permission", Mr. Eberts said.

„Mother is in Düsseldorf for the next two weeks but I know she would not object", I told him.

„Well, Peter, it is a matter of courtesy. You are a minor and you will actually work without pay. We do not want any trouble with the authorities, you understand."

„Yes, I do, Mr. Eberts. But then, who has to know?"

„I shall call her anyhow." He was quite serious about that He handed me the script.

„I know, you know it all by heart before it sinks into our old hats." He meant the dialogue. „I think we start on Friday, okay? Now, find your maid or aunt or whatever."

I took the script and went to the café to look for Annie. Until Friday, my nose was in the script. Walking through the house I memorised everybody's lines. It drove Annie bananas because she had to be my prompter and see that I was word perfect. I never did find out by the way if she had liked the performance. She probably dreamed through it all about her Joseph Wrath. Definitely, that was her highlight of Baden-Baden.

Rehearsing from scratch was not easy. The Eberts had not their rehearsal pat and held puppets in one hand and the script in the other. Then there was the scenery. The backdrops were easy, once hug in the right sequence from scene to scene, but Fräulein Becker and half of the stand-up scenery on her side and I had the other half. Besides the curtains, I had my side for the lights. A lot of blues for the night scenes, and yellow for the daylight. Playing with her golden ball, the Princess had to drop it into the well. She had to throw the ball into the air but it had to fall into the well, not next to it. It took great skill for Winny. I then had to be under the stage to put it into the frog's mouth. The right hand of the Princess had one string to move her arm, and the second long string also attached to her hand for the golden ball. The ball string ran through a small hole through the entire ball. When I put the ball into the frog's mouth, it had to have one half of the ball. But I worked in the dark and could only do it by feeling, otherwise when the frog appeared at the edge of the well and yanked his head while opening his mouth like throwing the ball back to her, the strings would have been twisted, and Winny would not have been able to pull the ball back into the hands of the Princess. Oh, but that was only one problem which needed a lot of rehearsing. As in the other plays, it was teamwork over and over again. I had only seconds after ball scene to scramble from under stage for the blackout while Fräulein Becker thundered away and put on a spotlight on the Prince. Now standing in all his glory next to the well. That meant I had to grope in the dark for the Prince from the side hook and put him quickly down into position because he was one part at least in that scene which was my responsibility, because Eberts had to work the Princess' nurse who witnessed the Prince and the Princess alone in the park. On and on it went, and I helped out with the dialogue constantly until the Eberts had it pat and had agreed on all the different voices for the different characters. Oh, there were a lot of arguments and sometimes a couple of quarrels as to what would be more suitable for each character. But finally, all the problems were resolved.

When Mother returned, Annie went back to Düsseldorf and Eberts came alone to the villa for coffee. After my first cup I was dismissed. I was very curious as to what these two were talking about, and I tried to eavesdrop behind the salon's doors, which were closest to where they were sitting. It was mostly Eberts talking about me. My talent, my devotion, my taking directions, my discipline. Well, he made me into a ‚wunderkind'! When I was called in, he had Mother convinced. She had consented. Finally, we had two complete run-throughs - as dress rehearsals are called in a live theatre. Then it was in the papers, „Our Premiere" on a Saturday, of course. The Eberts had sent special invitations to all their friends, among them many actors. But also to Mother and

Helen of whom I had seen very little of late, her father and Fräulein Erna. For once, the theatre was packed. Because of the three-act play, the variety show was limited to Mr. Kuno, the snake dancer and the Dolly Sisters. Backstage we were all nervous as hell. What made it worse was the outside noise of the audience. So many people knew each other and charted, we knew the house was packed. After the first act, great applause! We started to relax. Everything went like clockwork. Nobody made the slightest mistake. The applause was overwhelming at the end. Winny took me by the hand.

„Where are we going?" I asked surprised.

„Silly, it's Premiere, we are going to take a bow."

She went out first, we at her hand, then Herr Direktor and Fräulein Becker. The house lights were on and we bowed to our audience. Dieter, the usher, looked like a walking flower shop and passed out the bouquets. The audience cheered, and I heard many bravos. Dieter put a package in my hand, then we went backstage and hugged each other. But that was not the end. There was a small room separating us from the big theatre. The café had set up a buffet with coffee, cakes etc. for the Eberts and their friends. All the people on special invitations were there. Mother was in tears. This time tears of joy. She kissed me.

„It was lovely, Peter, so very lovely. To think my boy was involved in all that", she said.

Helen kissed my cheek. „You worked hard, I know, but what a success", she whispered into my ear.

Even Mr. Steiger was impressed. I think he saw me in a new light for the first time. It was a noisy coffee party. Everybody talking at the same time. My head was swimming. All these compliment. You would have thought I had done it all by myself. Mr. Eberts made a little speech that ended „but without our little Peter who's not so little anymore, we could not have managed", more applause. I turned red like a tomato and was very embarrassed.

„Don't eat too much cake, Peter", Mother said. „Tonight we dine on the grand terrace downstairs, just you and I. I have a window table for us."

Mrs. Eberts came over with a beautiful young lady and her mother. She introduced us to Mrs. Hester and her daughter Dorothy.

„Dorothy is an actress and my pupil, and I coach her", she informed us. „They live at the moment at the same hotel you used to live in."

We shook hands with Mrs. Hester, and Miss Dorothy took my hot face into her cool hands.

„So this is our young puppet player that Herr Direktor told me about", she smiled.

Oh God, she was beautiful. What wonderful blue eyes and all that lovely blond hair over her shoulder.

„I presently also perform, in a fairy tale, across the street in the old theatre. We play 'Snow White and The Seven Dwarfs' tomorrow", and with a glance to Mother, "and I hope you come to see me. I will leave the tickets at the box office for both of you."

I looked at Mother and nodded „Yes".

„Thank you very much, Miss Hester." Mother shook her hand.

„Don't forget to come backstage afterwards", she smiled and sailed away in a wonderful cloud of perfume.

„Well, my little chevalier, you seem to start early just like your father", Mother said.

The party started to break up. I gave my flowers to Winny. Dieter had given me a parcel but where had I put it? Oh, Mother had it in her hands. We said our goodbyes and went downstairs to the grand terrace.

„What a beautiful girl that Miss Hester is", Mother said, „and so kind to invite us tomorrow."

„Mother, how old could she be?"

„I think, eighteen or nineteen, maybe", she answered.

„Mother, I think I am in love."

„Unfortunately, a little too old for you, my son", she laughed.

The grand terrace was very elegant and so was the clientele. Some ladies in long dresses wore expensive furs. Most of the gentlemen in dark suit some even in dinner jackets. The menu here had a rich choice of different foods. Food rationing had recently been introduced. Mother left most of our stamps in the hotel, as much as to cover the luncheons. At night we usually had a sandwich at home. The stamps were only good for the town you lived in, but for business people, there were travelling stamps, accepted everywhere in Germany, and Father had sent us an envelope full of them. That night she used the travelling stamps.

„You must be ver hungry, Peter, eat what you like, I will even buy you a glass of wine with Father's permission. Yes, he phoned today and sends his love to you. Things are dreadful there. They practically live underground in those bunkers night after night. Of course, if you look around here, you would never know."

Music started to play, some couples danced. Dinner was wonderful, the service excellent. What an exciting day it had been. When we were back at the villa I opened the parcel.

„It arrived this morning in the mail", Mother said.

I threw the outer wrapping away. „Look, there is a note attached." She was as curious as I. It was from Annie and read: „Dear Peter, I hope your performance was a success. I send you an old friend, slightly damaged unfortunately. I wanted to give it to you on Christmas day but was afraid your Dad might not approve. It was found in the rubble after the fire. Fondly, your Annie."

I unwrapped the package. It was Helga, my celluloid doll

with a big hole in her head. Sunday, Mother went to church with me. Afterwards we picked our tickets and went to the hotel. On passing Mrs. and Miss Hester's table, we thanked them again for the tickets. The old theatre was a little jewel box. She had given us seats in the first row.

Miss Dorothy was „Snow White". Gone was the blond hair. But even with a black wig she looked breathtaking. It was an enchanting performance. At the curtain call, Miss Dorothy winked at me. I was like a colleague of hers. It made me very proud. Mother did not want to go backstage, it was not her world, or she was too shy, I didn't know why.

„You run along, just make an excuse for me. See you later at home", she said.

I went and gave my name to the concierge who checked his list and pointed to a door. I went through a small corridor, the staircase to my right, and found the stage. Most actors were still standing around talking. There it was again, that special smell of grease paint that I had smelled backstage at „Hänsel and Gretel". Miss Dorothy saw me and came towards me with outstretched arms.

„Peter, sweetheart, you did come", she said. I made an excuse for Mother which she did not comment on, but introduced me around as a little friend who had a Premiere yesterday at the marionette theatre. The „Evil Queen" turned out to be a very nice lady. The dwarfs were much smaller than I and had very old faces. They were all Lilliputians. Miss Dorothy showed me around. She pointed stage right to a small spiral staircase on top of which was a big stage light.

„When you come again", she said, „you go up there just under the light. There is a seat from which you can see the stage and backstage. Just wait for me, I'll change quickly and then I will take you to a café house for an ice cream where all the artists meet."

After a while, the real Miss Dorothy appeared, and we left the theatre but not before she said to the concierge, George, „This is Peter. He works with the Eberts, and is a friend of mine, so let him in when he comes."

Just before the old part of town was the café. A tiny garden in front for the summer. The place was fairly full, and it seemed everybody knew Miss Dorothy. One man called and said, „Hey, Miss Dorothy, your dwarfs are getting taller by the day!" That amused the others and they laughed. Miss Dorothy stuck her tongue out at him. She took a table just for the two of us and ordered ice cream.

„You see, Peter, we all belong to the Frankfurt Theatre. I am only here for two months, but how heavenly to be away from the big city."

Her father had been killed in action, so now it was only she and her mother.

„Of course, after three weeks we have to leave the hotel. Mother is already looking for rooms for the rest of our stay. I am just fresh out of acting school, and „Snow White" is my first big part."

I told her how I admired her performance. That seemed to please her greatly.

„Well, Peter, it will take me a while to get up there but at least I was accepted into the Frankfurt Theatre. Well, it's not Berlin yet, but who knows, maybe one day." She chatted on.

„And the movies, you are so beautiful, Miss Dorothy", I said.

Her big blue eyes went to the ceiling. „Yes, the movies. My dream, of course. But fat chance to be discovered in little Baden-Baden."

I escorted her back to the hotel. She put her arm through mine. God, I was proud. For me she was a star. She made me feel grown up and talked to me like I was one of them.

I thanked her for the ice cream and the tickets once again. She waved goodbye and went in.

Finally, I was in class B with Fräulein Dump. She was a fat old lady. Perhaps around sixty. Because of her name, she had a nickname immediately, ‚Dumpfnudel'. Actually, a delectable Austrian dessert well known over the border. A heavenly white dough with a vanilla sauce. She, of course, was just the opposite. Old and fat, she also had a stick, just like that old goat. But she was much cleverer. Her love was music. I am still convinced of that. She played the flute and made us sing. I must say, at least not Hitler songs. However, she never mastered her instrument although she tried very hard. But the poor old dear just could not do it, as much as she tried. Well at one time she was fluting away and blew so many wrong notes that I started to giggle.

„Jaqulay, did you laugh at me?" she shouted. I stood up. „Yes, Mrs. Dump."

„Come forward." Palms out, she hit me with that bamboo stick on top of my fingertips on both hands. It hurt just as well but that was her trick - it didn't show.

Naturally, from then on I hated school. But there were many more schools to come. I always was a medium student. Nothing to write home about, but at least I had never to repeat a class. With local boys I did not make friends. They were just too different. Nobody lived in a villa. And nobody ate in a hotel. But somehow they all knew where I lived and where I ate. They had never seen the marionette theatre or a real live show. I was outside their circle and I knew it. And with all my activities it did not bother me at all.

When I turned ten years old, I had to join the Hitler movement. Well, Mother and I got the costume together and I was off to my first official training course. The leader could not have been older than Miss Dorothy. He was a very good-looking boy. Black hair and steely blue eyes. Once we were lined up, he asked who was going to church on Sunday. I put my hand up and he made a note in a little black book. After left turn, right turn training, we played robbers, and when somebody nailed him to the ground, which meant he had lost. We were all wearing leather short pants, but he wore no underwear, and I could see his big balls and big dick. It excited me very much. Unfortunately, the drill was on Saturdays, which interfered with the theatre. I pleaded with Mother to send them a letter of excuse because of illness. My dear mother obliged. On with the theatre but only for three weeks, when a handsome guy showed up at the villa with a piece of paper that I had to show up for duty. Mother, of course, was upset.

„I can't write more notes of excuse", she explained.

I had a little talk with the leader about this matter, knowing I was already in his little black book.

„Well", he told me, „we will now be soliciting for the poor in winter." He handed me a round red box with a swastika on it. „Go and collect. If you should collect the most for the next month, I will excuse you from Saturday's exercises."

He grinned an evil smile. Did he really know how beautiful he was? I doubted it. And he doubted I would return with one Mark. In my uniform, entering the hotel, I ran into Mr. Steiger.

„Ah, you're in the Hitler movement now. A new step in your life. Congratulations." He shook my hand. When he was gone, I went straight to the concierge, Mr. Eberhard.

„Please, Mr. Eberhard, I have a very strange request, and please help me", I said.

„Mr. Jaqulay, what is it that you want?" He looked curious.

Ah, now I was Mr. Jaqulay. How every interesting, I thought.

„I have to collect for the poor in winter. Could you do me a favour and let no other boy in to collect, just me?"

He smiled. „Of course, Mr. Jaqulay. You grew up here. I will throw the others out. „

„Oh, Mr. Eberhard, I thank you. It will save me hours." I shook his hand and Mr. Eberhard stuck to our agreement. As much as Mother hated it, but from that day I had to wear the brown shirt, black tie held by a leather knot at the top. Pants and shoes were optional. After all, I was just a ‚pimpf'. It was the lowest and youngest rank in the Hitler movement. Mother sat down for luncheon every day looking out of the window, not trying to see me collecting. But I went every day from table to table. Many faces I knew, and they knew me, of course. The strangers I had to talk to. But by my reassurance they would never be bothered again, they opened their wallets. Well, in the hotel there were no nickels and dimes, but bills ranging from one Mark to five Marks. The whole procedure took an hour, and luncheon had to wait until I returned with my red box to our table. The whole thing annoyed my mother but I had told her about the deal with my leader, and she understood that Saturdays were sacred to me. What a good sport she was. When I went to my beautiful leader, he had the same evil smile on his face.

„Well, pimpf Jaqulay, let's see what you have collected."

He took the red box out of my hands and shook it.

„Ah, our church goer. I don't hear anything clink. Probably you are returning an empty box."

He broke the seal and opened it anyhow. Out came all that paper money. The ones and fives. His face froze and he stared to add it up. It came over three hundred Marks. I felt very cocky because I knew the other boys in the streets could not have got that kind of money.

„Okay, you win." He put something down excusing me from Saturday's exercises.

„Peter, I don't know how you did it but for the Führer, try to do it again", he said.

Not smiling because I knew instinctively that he did not like me because I was not as athletic as he was.

„I will, my leader. I will do my best for the Führer."

I stood at attention.

„Relax", he said, „did anyone ever tell you that you have beautiful eyes?"

„Get out of here!" he yelled after me as I ran out. However, to be quite sure that Saturdays were really mine, I solicited the dining room for three months, time after time. I had no more trouble with the Baden-Baden Hitler youth. However, Mother had to take a photo of me in uniform, maybe for Father, I never found out.

„Der Platterhof"

Up in the hills above Berchtesgaden was a grand hotel in the most elegant Bavarian style. Decorated with exquisite sculptures and paintings. All these antique items actually belonged to various museums. They were requisitioned for the interiors by the Führer because his hotel was his „guest house", not far from his own ‚Berghof'.

However, a selected, much screened public was allowed to rent rooms. The Maître de Restaurant had worked for the Meyers in Düsseldorf. Through him, my father rented adjoining rooms for himself and I for two weeks. Mother had very much wanted to be in Düsseldorf to supervise repairs on the house. God only knows why, the war was not finished for a long time to come.

This trip with my father alone was a total novelty to me as it was our first trip together. The view of the Alps was breathtaking. It was summering, the meadows dotted with blue gentian and yellow dandelion. The air was full of the smell of freshly mowed grass. Both our rooms had spectacular views over the mountains. The style of architecture was new to me. „So, this is Bavaria." I loved the houses with their balconies, overflowing with bright red, hanging geraniums, a profusion of colours. Never had I seen houses painted with large murals on the outside. The subjects mostly religious, this art was called „Flügelmalerei". The actually small windows looked large because of the elaborate frames painted around them on the walls of the buildings. Altogether, mountains, the large meadows, the colourful houses, gave the impression of a fairy tale book. In those days, many Bavarians still wore their native costumes I was not familiar with. The ladies were dressed in „Dirndls", the men in knee length „Lederhosen", and their hats with the big „Gamsbart" were very amusing to me. The food, that is the native food, was different, too. I remember especially their dumplings, which came in many delicious variations, and through my life became a great favourite of mine.

Gregarious Father soon made friends in the hotel. There was a couple from Berlin, a couple from Hamburg, and a single gentleman, a professor, but a young one and very jolly. I liked him the best. I think because of Father's suggestion who knew that mathematics were my weak spot, he taught me while hiking and we hiked a lot. He taught me well which later in school was to my advantage. But why all that hiking with people from big cities who were accustomed to sitting in cars? Well, they wanted to see the „Berghof", but no matter what cable car we took to what mountain, it was by then very camouflaged. Much later, I found out, it actually was very near the Platterhof.

The Eagle's Nest, Hitler's famous teahouse, however, was in full view on a mountain behind the hotel.

Also Göring's villa could be seen from afar, and quite often we saw Mrs. Göring and her daughter taking a walk. One night there was great excitement in the hotel. The Führer himself would arrive. By nine p.m. he had not arrived, and Father sent me to bed. Next morning, he explained, „We waited until midnight, no show, instead six whores arrived from Munich, and a little later came Ciano from Italy."

Father was quite disappointed, I could tell. „Whores", who are they? I had visions of black veiled ladies in mourning. Father in his frustration had forgotten that he was talking to his little son. Typically, he left it to the professor to clue me in, which he did with great relish having been there, too. So I learned not only mathematics but also about ladies of the night and about some history on Count Ciano and his entertainment provided for him in Hitler's „guest house". Before we left, soldiers started to camouflage the Platterhof. It started with the large terraces in white marble, onto which they shovelled black graffiti.

A few weeks later, Hitler declared the total war. I did not know what that meant but I soon found out. The hotel was closed down, and Miss Dorothy and her mother had left. The legitimate theatres were closed. Thank God, they left us out of all that. All the hotels were converted into war hospitals. The casino was closed first. Baden-Baden emptied very quickly. The parks were not kept up anymore. Our clientele dwindled so that the Eberts closed that too. It was a great shock for me when they called Mother, and she related the news to me. There was a final meeting where the Eberts gave me al lovely volume of puppets and marionette plays inscribed, and a photo of Winny and Herr Direktor with the snake dancer. It was one of my saddest moments so far, saying goodbye to those lovely people, the marionettes and all. Eberts and Winny gave me a Balinese hand puppet. A very graceful figurine. I liked it a lot, but one of the marionettes I played with would have been so much greater. Later I found out that all the figurines were only consignment to them, so they could not give any away. It was a very tearful goodbye, needless to say. A chapter of my young life was closed forever. Baden-Baden became a dead town. It was heartbreaking to see it all go down hill.

One night at 3 p.m. Father arrived. He had just listened to the BBC in London, which was not allowed, of course, in Germany. He knew about the successful landing of the Allies and wanted us closer to Düsseldorf, since we were just half an hour from the French border. All night long we packed our belongings like a bunch of wild people and stored it in his little Opel and on top. Next morning we left after saying goodbye to Mr. Steiger and Helen. I gave Helen a kiss and promised to come back. Tears rolled down my cheeks. It was all so sudden for me. A definite chapter had closed, and now what? We drove without lights during the night in the Autobahn. The trip seemed endless and we went into the Sauerland which turned out as sour as its sounds. Father had got two rooms in an inn for us to sit out the war. Finally, by daybreak we arrived in a little miserable farmer's village about hundred kilometres from Düsseldorf. It stank to high heaven with all the manure in front of the houses. We stopped at a house covered from top to bottom with slate. In the light it had a fearful appearance. It was a corner building. The sign advertised some German beer, but of course the light was out. Father rang the bell. Mr. Dick, our new landlord, opened the door. He was in his middle thirties, and I wondered what kept him from active duty. He looked healthy enough to me. It turned out he had a hernia and flat feet. Besides him, there was Mrs. Müller, also an involuntary exile. Mr. Müller was a soldier but it did not take me long to figure out their relationship. The whole thing was a big bore including school.

This time girls and boys were in one class. I stood out like a sore thumb in my Baden-Baden finery but at that point I did not care one bit. It was such a low class, and ugly after Baden-Baden. I hated it all so much that I have never returned. The only fun was a play the school put on, and guess that was the star! The bombs came closer, and one hit a house in which a girl I went to school with lived with her family. They all suffocated. All the children were made to visit the neighbours' house and view the six dead people on open caskets. It was a nightmare for me. I dreamed about it for years. I suppose, it was propaganda to show us the gruesomeness of the enemy. One girl from class was also from Düsseldorf. She and I, her mother and my mother made friends easily and saw a lot of each other. Her name was Beatrice. A real tomboy. We would steal tobacco from Mr. Dick and roll cigarettes in the attic and smoke. Finally, May came around. The farmers and their help went into the fields. The streets were empty, and everywhere there was a peaceful silence. On a day like this it was hard to believe there was a war, and that the Allies were coming closer and closer. Two days before, the pace had another one. With the hustle and bustle German soldiers with arms and tanks had come through our village from the front line. But they had gone and no one knew where. Maybe they were still in the hills. One could not be sure. All we knew was that the Allies were approaching. The village was waiting. Most of the people were relieved that soon the war would be over for them. I was in school, and it was after lunch when our teacher dismissed us without giving any explanation. She only said, „Get home as quickly as possible." She really did not have to tell us why. We knew this would be „the day". Nervously, laughing and giggling we went out of the school and down the hill, glad that class had finished so early for the day. There was great deal of excitement in the air.

Expectations of things to come ran high. The most fantastic rumours were going around about the approaching troops. My mother was waiting for me. The inn was a large building facing the main street. Two trees stood in front of the house on either side of the staircase that led to the entrance. Mother was scared. A friend had called from the next village. American troops had just reached it, and in about fifteen minutes they would be at our doors. I looked out of the window. No German troops were in the village. No fighting. That was Mother's only comfort. Everyone in the house was almost hysterical with fright. The innkeeper came running into our living room and urged us to go down to the cellar. I think he was afraid, the first tank would blast his inn into eternity. People in the streets were running home, or to relatives. Some came to our house because we had a good shelter. Then quite suddenly the village was deathly quiet. It was a frightful silence, and the air was heavy with suspense. No one said a word. Only by the moving lips of some women could I tell that they were praying. It was dark in the shelter. Only one small window above street level sent in some sunrays from that beautiful day outside. I peeped through it. In front of me was a deserted street, and then suddenly I saw at the very end the first tank slowly rounding the corner coming towards us. A gigantic machine with its gun pointed straight into my face.

„Do you see anything, my darling?" Mother asked.

„They are here, Mother, I can see the first tank", I said.

They tried to get me away from the window but I resisted and pulled back.

„If only Father was with us, oh God! What will they do to us? Here we are save from the bombings, and now we will be killed for sure", she whimpered.

„They will not harm women and children, but they surely will kill me", said the innkeeper. He was crouched in a corner on his knees, his face hidden in his hands. „They will think I am a soldier. You must tell them that I was never in the war. I am a sick man."

I ducked under the window. Now I could hear as the noise grew louder and I dared look again. There the tank was, right in front of our house. It tried to get around the corner but did not quite make it and ran into one of the trees and the staircase which it crushed to pieces under its weight. The whole house shook. The little windows splintered into a thousand parts and dust and debris came through it and filled my lungs, so I had to cough. Mother clasped her hands on front of my mouth in order that I could not be heard outside. The women screamed and ran to the opposite side of the shelter.

„Quiet, please be quiet. Maybe they will not find us", warned the innkeeper. The tank backed up and stopped. I could now hear the muffled voices of the soldiers. Strange voices. Strange language. They climbed off the tank and entered the house shouting. Mother was standing against the wall opposite the entrance, and I in front of her. No one dared move. My heart was beating so hard, I thought my chest would burst. Then we heard the cellar door open and the sound of boots descending. It sounded like five or six men. They searched the cellar, and then the shelter door flung open, and in they came with their guns in front of them pointing them straight at Mother and me. They looked about but saw no German soldiers, only our frightened group. I could tell from their dusty faces that they were relieved. They even smiled at us and shouted to the innkeeper „Wine, wine!"

That we all understood! And on that thirsty note the spell was broken. The innkeeper with his hands over his head went upstairs. The housekeeper behind him in the same fashion of surrender. The rest of us following. More tanks and cars were rolling by the house. The bar room filled up quickly with soldiers, tall, slender young Americans and all so thirsty. The farmers came out of the houses to watch the endless flow of tanks and cars. I was standing on the rest of our staircase. It was a sight to see. The soldiers were sunning themselves lying on „Steppdecken", a special kind of comforters used in bedrooms, usually in bright colours that looked just too funny on a tank. They threw chocolate and candy to us children, and I soon found myself on the ground collecting all of those marvellous things we had not tasted for years. The excitement amongst the people grew after those tense hours, everybody laughing and enjoying themselves, and the general mood turned into a gay carnival atmosphere. After all, the war had come to an end for us fast. There were so many new and strange things to see like powdered milk packed in little aluminium bags. Chewing gum, something completely different to us. Soon, all the children were chewing, and Mother said to them that I looked like a cow the way I was moving my jaws. Wine turned out to be the object of trade with, and in exchange we got coffee and more chocolate for me. Mother traded one good bottle of wine for a bar of soap and immediately disappeared into the bathroom where I could hear her sing joyfully while she cleaned herself with the luxurious foam that had been missing from German bathrooms for so long. The inn had a small ballroom, rather dilapidated since it had not been used during the war. Twenty soldiers declared it now as their temporary bedroom. There was a piano in there. The young GI sat down and played beautifully Chopin and Bach. Soon, everybody in the house stood around and listened. After a while I got bored and sneaked out. Turning into the back yard I saw some feathers in the ground which was odd. So I made my way to the goose stall at the end of the yard where we kept two geese because of meat rations. Sure enough, the gate was open and our geese were gone. I ran back into the house. Before I entered I caught a glimpse of those two dear animals dangling down from a tank.

„Mother!" I cried, „they stole our geese!"

The piano playing stopped, and a most uncomfortable pianist, his face red like a tomato, tried to leave the ballroom quietly. Knowing how much the Germans like good music, he had us all around the piano while his buddies went into the backyard and killed the geese. Mother was very angry and let out the young GI have it, and he was lucky not to understand German. She took him outside pointing to the geese and balled out his partners in crime. Cooking facilities on the tank however, if any, are more than inadequate and so they made a truce. Mother would prepare the meal and offer some more wine. The GIs would contribute the coffee, milk and more soap for mother. And we would all feast on the two birds. That evening, I became violently ill. All the chocolates, sweets and a heavy meal were just too much. Mother finally grabbed me and ordered me to bed. While I got ready, I heard her talk to Mrs. Müller, they were giggling. The door was ajar, and Mother said, „Oh, come on, I don't believe it"

„Well go to the attic and look for yourself", Mrs. Müller said.

„They are hanging there to dry, I made him wash them. Can you imagine a big man like him to be so afraid?"

„But what did happen?" Mother enquired.

„Well, he told me", she giggled, „just at the moment when the soldiers came into the shelter, he really thought they would kill him. Such a coward, that innkeeper."

„Well", still laughing, Mother excused herself, „I'll see that my boy went to bed. He over-indulged himself today, just like he used to at Christmas. But I let him; after all it was an important day for all of us. I'll be right down."

I was in bed already, all my treasures piled up on the night table. Mother came in and kissed me goodnight, and I fell asleep very quickly.

James Russel was a very tall Negro. His home was Brooklyn, and he had been fighting in Europe since the invasion. After the long day he was deadly tired and was looking forward to the makeshift beds in the ballroom of the inn. That evening, James felt deeply depressed. His long time buddy had been killed in action just a few days before, and for two weeks he had no word from his wife and his little boy. He just could not face joining the crowd. On his own, he started to explore the house. Up he went the narrow staircase. The first room he looked into was an old fashioned bathroom. Not any different from home, he thought, but so much cleaner. Every room he inspected was simple and clean. The last door led him into a nice little living room, which was ours. He put the light on. It was a small room but cheerful and cosy. Opposite the window was another room, the door slightly ajar. James looked inside. It was dark. He found the light switch next to the door. I must have been asleep for half an hour, and so when I woke up, the lights were on. There was this Negro GI standing in the doorway. Naturally, I was afraid, to wake up and find a stray soldier staring at you is scary. But what really frightened me most, was that he was black and absolutely gigantic. I wanted to scream and I thought I did, but no sound escaped my mouth. I grabbed my blanket and pulled it up to my nose, peering at him. Somehow the blanket gave me a sense of security. I heard about dark people before and even had seen pictures but I had never seen one in the flesh. By now, I was awake, and after a moment I could feel how ill at ease the Negro was. Adults can be so very embarrassed when confronted with a frightened child, especially when they know that they are the cause. I sensed that he had come in by mistake, obviously thinking the room was empty. I lowered the blanket a little. The Negro smiled and said something I could not understand. He raised his big hand to his neck making a motion of a knife cutting his throat I understood. He was asking me if I was afraid that he might kill me. Slowly I nodded. He smiled again and shook his head repeating „No, no". He came closer, still smiling, and perhaps because of that good-natured smile I suddenly wasn't afraid anymore.

„James", he said. And now I pointed to myself and said „Peter".

He stretched out his big black hand, and I noticed a gold ring with a big red stone. We shook hands. He sat down on my bed trying to tell me with big gestures about his little boy at home. He mimicked so well and in such a funny way that I had to laugh. With his big eyes rolling towards the ceiling and his hands folded in prayer making all sorts of war noises, then cutting through the air with a flat hand, he indicated the he too wished this mad war would come to an end. Suddenly he reached into his pocket, and in his big black hand he held a golden fruit. It looked like an apple to me but much bigger and more round. He gave it to me. When I bit into it, he laughed and took it back to show me how to peel it. The segments of the fruit were delicious and tasted very sweet I liked it very much and thanked him. The Negro pointed to the fruit, „orange", he said, and then cupping his hand behind his ear made me repeat it.

„Orange", I said, and ate the rest of it.

I asked him if he belonged to the soldiers staying in the house, which he did not understand, since I asked him in German. It took al lot of pointing and mimicking on my part to get the idea across to him. Then he understood and nodded. It had been a very complicated conversation and we both broke out into laughter. He still carried his gun with him, and I was just dying to handle it. If just for a while, so I pointed to the gun. He got up, thinking I was still afraid of it. But I got him be the sleeve saying „No, no". Pointing to the gun again and then to myself. He shook his head but

I clapped my hands together asking him please let me have it for a while. For a moment a very thoughtful expression came across his face. He then emptied the gun and handed it to me putting the ammunition on the night table. I examined it carefully and tried to make out as if I was shooting out the window but obviously I was doing it wrong. He sat behind me and showed me how to put the bolster against my shoulder and how to take aim. We were so engrossed in the technique of shooting, me aiming at the door, that we did not hear my mother enter. She took one step from the door towards the bed and stood frozen. All the colour had left her face. She looked terrified from me to the GI. The Negro, surprised by her appearance, jumped up, the gun in his hands. Now there they stood, both afraid, and he looking down at little mother. It struck me so funny I had to laugh. Shyly I pulled on his sleeve, pointing mischievously at the ammunition on the night table.

„Are you all right?" Mother whispered. „Did he hurt you?"

„I'm fine, Mother. Don't worry, he is ver nice, and he doesn't mean any harm."

I tried to calm her. Mother relaxed a little and smiled rather forcibly at the tall tower of a man in front of her. James made a little bow.

„Auf vie doer zane", he said patting my cheek. „Good little boy."

With that he left the room and we heard him going downstairs. Mother ran to the living room door and locked it tightly.

„I know it is my fault", she explained, „I should not have left the room with all the soldiers in the house."

„But, Mother, please calm down. I was not afraid at all", I lied. „And look what he gave me." Triumphantly, I showed her a handful of orange peels. „You never tasted anything

like it", I went on. „It's called orange and grows in America."
Mother kissed me on the forehead, „I know, darling, we
used to be able to buy the same things, too. They are very
good for little boys but because of the war, you have never
had one before."

She had tears in her eyes, which I could not quite understand. „There is still so much you have not seen but some
day, who knows, as soon as the war is really over, a new
world will open up for you. Who knows, maybe even you
will visit the land where the oranges come from."

After all the excitement of the day, I fell asleep quickly,
only to be awakened once more by Mother. She was in her
nightgown and wore her hairnet, so I gathered that she too
had been asleep. There was a lot of noise downstairs. I could
hear the soldiers shouting from the street and the sound of
gunfire.

„Quickly!" she said, dragging me out of bed and taking me
by the hand, pulling me through the living room. „The German soldiers must have come back during the night. They
are fighting in the streets!"

We ran downstairs, I've never seen my mother run so
fast. The last American soldiers were leaving by the front
door. Then down the cellar staircase into the safety of the
shelter. The innkeeper, Mrs. Müller and several other people were already there, offering a rather grotesque picture
in their various nightgowns. We all sat crouched on a long
bench, again not knowing what was in store for us this
time. Because of the broken window and the silence of the
night, every step, shout or shot could be heard very clearly.
Sometimes the fighting was near the house. Sometimes it
seemed further away. Drowsy as I was, I sat on Mother's lap
and tried to sleep. After an hour the fighting stopped. Only
with great persuasion by the women would the innkeeper
go upstairs to check the situation. He finally gathered all his

courage and went. A little later he returned. The fighting had stopped and we could go back to bed.

„The Germans have left the village", he announced.

Going up into the hall, I saw some of the American soldiers returning and suddenly the door was pushed wide open. Two GIs carried a soldier on a makeshift stretcher. Someone had spread a blanket over the body and only his shoes could be seen.

„One of them got killed", whispered the innkeeper. The first GI carrying the stretcher tripped, and I saw a black hand slipping from under the blanket. In a flash, I saw the big gold ring with the red stone.

„Mama", I cried, „it's James, mama, they killed him!"

We were cut off from the rest of the world. No newspapers, no telegrams, and no telephone service. What had happened to Father? Where was he, was the daily question. It practically drove my mother out of her mind.

A month later, out of the blue, Father arrived to take us home. God, were we happy. We packed up again in super speed; we could not wait to get home. I was eleven then and ready to go back to the big city and leave the miserable village behind.

On arrival, Annie was there and a female cousin of hers on a visit. We all had our hands full to get the house in order as quickly was possible. Dad was busy in the factory. Lisa and Aunt Ellie lived close by. We saw a lot of them. School had not opened, and I made more puppets and built my own little theatre in the burned out attic. Lisa knew my passion for theatrics and often helped me, especially after I mastered Father's movie camera and started to film my performances. The trains were not running, therefore the bike came in very handy. There was no reason to drive into town, Düsseldorf was sad, destroyed, and with people trying to clear the rubble and save the bricks if they were still in one piece.

Klaus who still lived across the street, Lisa and I, for a short time, opened in an abandoned garage a little theatre and played for the children of the neighbourhood. It was all right but not the same thing as it used to be. Life was sad and hard. The food shortage was the worst Father's old clothes were altered for me because I began to grow rather fast.

When school opened again, we gave up our little theatre. The class was mixed again, boys and girls. Instead of Heil Hitler, we had to pray before class started. Our lady teacher, Fräulein Ruth, had a good sense of humour and was very popular. There were ten of us who wanted to go to high school. „Gymnasium" in German. She prepared us after regular school hours for the exams were to take in order to be accepted. From now on it was studying, day in, day out. Sometimes I took the bike and visited Father at the factory. He had an attractive office, more like a large living room connecting to Uncle Joe's office. The doorman knew me as well as Father's secretary who had a little office before Father's. I would wave to her and she would wave back, then I would knock on Father's door and he pressed a button on his desk to release the door. On one of those visits, Father opened the door by hand, continuing to talk to someone in his office. A very beautiful lady sat in an armchair, elegantly dressed with a large hat on.

„Gudrun, this is my son, Peter", he said to her. She smiled and stretched her hand out. I shook hers and bowed.

„You know", he used the familiar term ‚Du', „he played in Baden-Baden in the marionette theatre. He was only a little boy then. But soon he is going to high school." Father said to her. She was still smiling at me. I noticed her white gloves, which I had not seen on a lady since Baden-Baden. She then got up, picked up her handbag. She was as tall as Father was.

„Martin, I'll let you two alone now. I'll call you later", she said to my father. „It was very nice meeting you finally, Peter. I've seen photos of you. We shall meet again", she left.

„Mrs. Greff is in the art business, friend of Mr. Glotz'. We will visit him on Sunday", Father explained.

The exams were the following week, and Father drummed into me how important it was to be accepted. On the way home, I thought about the beautiful Mrs. Greff. It struck me odd that they were on a first name basis, they called each other ‚Du' instead of ‚Sie'. But then I forgot all about it until Sunday when we visited Mr. Glotz. He also lived in a half bombed out house. It was a Victorian building in the centre of town and must have been very grand in its day. He greeted me heartily and introduced his housekeeper who he ordered to bring apple juice for me and champagne for his guests. She served it in the living room where Mrs. Greff was waiting.

„Hello, you two", she beamed, „great that you are here." We all toasted to better times to come. Mr. Glotz had a beautiful painting collection in which he dealt. I wandered around and looked at them all. Later came Mrs. Meyer and her husband whom I had never met.

„Peter", she hugged me, „how you have grown. This is my husband Mr. Meyer." We shook hands.

„My wife told me that you went to school together with my daughter in the Sauerland", he said. Then they all gave a big hello to Mrs. Greff. Fred Glotz liked company and was a very good host. I had a plate full of delicious cookies and all before lunch! It was clear they all knew each other very well, and I would learn later that my father had an enormous circle of friends and was very popular. They talked about the bad times; Düsseldorf was occupied by the British then. Father was itching to go fishing and hunting - two of his great hobbies. But it was impossible to get a licence, let alone fire arms.

„I met this British colonel who hunts", Mr. Meyer said. „I'll introduce you, Mr. Jaqulay, and maybe he can arrange something."

„Oh, nothing would please me more", Father said enthusiastically.

They made a date in our house for the next week. Mother had lunch ready when we came back from our Sunday drink. After lunch, Father took a nap; he always did for two hours, even during the week.

I told Mother about the house, the paintings and Mr. Glotz' hospitality. I gave her the greeting from him and the Meyers.

„Was there a Mrs. Greff there, too?" she asked me.

„Oh yes, the beautiful Mrs. Greff."

„Had you met her before?" Mother asked.

„Just once, briefly at Father's office", I said.

„She was a very good friend of Mr. Glotz", Mother mused.

„I think so, they are on first name basis and call each other ‚Du'", I told her.

„You mean Fred Glotz and Mrs. Greff?"

„No, also Father and Mrs. Greff", I said.

Mother fell silent for a long time.

Mrs. Gudrun Greff was the quintessential beauty that Hitler adored. She was tall and slender, with perfect long legs. Lots of genuine blond hair and large light blue eyes shaded by brown long lashes. She came from a modest German family; her father sold coal to private homes. She had married a successful photographer who was immediately drafted into the army as a front-line photographer when war broke out. They had known each other for a short time only when they married in a hurry because of his war duties. When they saw each other, it was on leave. He was originally from Berlin and it was there that they met. Two years later he was killed in action. Gudrun was then a sales lady in a top speciality store for ladies' and men's' hats. She had waited on my father but they met at the house of the art dealer Glotz who also bought his hats there, and had taken a great fancy to the young widow. Glotz was single, rich and a great womaniser. Eventually, his house, which also housed its gallery, became very infamous, so those mothers from good families forebode their daughters to attend his parties. Bold-headed, fat Glotz was no beauty. He was a great host and raconteur. He also had storage rooms full of goodies, then very desirable to the girls. You name it, from silk stockings to lovely cheap jewellery. It was not uncommon for him to invite the entire female ballet from the Operetta Theatre. At more formal parties, he needed a hostess, besides his cook and housekeeper. He had chosen on occasions Gudrun who had agreed because in his house she had a chance to meet the rich. She actually hated him because of his constant advances after those long dinner parties. In that house, she met my father who fell head over heels in love with her. Glotz, of course, notices, and for a short time the men did not talk to each other. When Glotz realised that Father was serious about the affair, he slowly relented and they all made up. By then, Gudrun had quit her job, and Father rented for her space in a flatware shop, where she sold bronze figurines, ash trays and all that junk. She knew the artists, Father was able to get her the metals and after a short time she did well in her new „art" business. Father was in love and showered the most expensive gifts on her. He took her everywhere but the focal place was still Mr. Glotz' villa and / or a certain elegant night spot called „Bar Charlotte". No wonder, because the manageress Ena was Gudrun's best friend and the owner, Mr. Paul, went hunting with Father. Quickly, all of Düsseldorf knew that Father had a mistress. Some gents regretted that fact very much because of earlier trysts with her but from then on it was „hands off Gudrun".

The day of the exams, I was a nervous wreck. I bicycled into town to the new school. The courtyard was full with boys of my age. I spotted Klaus who was just as nervous as I. The letters from A to Y were strung on a line, and we had to form behind the letter of our last name. The teacher did a little reshuffling until he had twelve boys in one line. The classroom was large. Each applicant had a desk to himself - no cheating here, I thought. A teacher appeared, and we all received a pad and a pencil.

„You now have thirty minutes to write a story, let's say about your last vacation, or your family, or whatever you wish. But the story must have an ending and be written out at least three pages."

The pads were large. The teacher looked at his watch and said „Go!" what a story to write. I saw others trying to think the same thing. Well, a quick decision had to be made, and I told the story about our disastrous Christmas cake.

„Stop!" I heard the teacher say. But I had finished in time. He collected the sheets with our names on top, of course, and left. Another teacher appeared. He went to the blackboard and quickly wrote some figures on it. Mathematics, my weak spot.

„You have fifteen minutes to solve it."

He sat behind his desk. I worked as well as I could but was not sure at all if the result would be right.

„Stop!" And again he collected the papers. Someone else appeared and wrote a chart down on which names of rivers were written.

„Fifteen minutes", he said. „Copy the names of the rivers and write the country behind each one."

Some of them belonged to Germany. But I knew the Nabe,

the Rhine, the Volga, etc. It seemed the time just would not pass. A short essay about a person in history, Adolf Hitler and the Third Reich excluded, of course. I chose Marie Antoinette. I knew a lot about her because I had read one of Mother's books. Finally, an eternity later we were dismissed. The results we would learn from our local teacher, Fräulein Ruth, in a few days. A few days! Suspense would kill us all. I bicycled home as fast as I could. God, was it great to escape that classroom.

At lunch, Mother and Father asked simultaneously, „Did you pass?"

„The results are given out in a few days", I told them. I could tell they were now as anxious as I was.

„Well, let's hope for the best", Father said.

After lunch, Father took his usual nap. Two days later, after school prayers, Fräulein Ruth sat down looking very serious, in front of her a stack of papers.

„Three of you did not make it", she announced. You could have heard a pin drop.

„I shall read you the names of those applicants who came through."

She started to read names as I counted. My God, she was at five, not I. Number 6, not I. My throat started to close. Number seven, Peter Jaqulay, of course! She grinned at me wickedly. She had made me last on purpose.

„By the way, Peter, Marie Antoinette's lover was Swedish, not Danish." Well, Fräulein Ruth was a spinster; it had been her game. All hell broke loose. She was pleased that seven in her class had passed, and we went home shouting like crazy.

„We did it! We did it!"

My parents were very pleased. Father gave me fifty Marks. Mother was on the phone to tell Aunt Ellie and Uncle Joe and Lisa. The next day was a Friday. Fräulein Ruth lined us seven in front of her desk.

„Well, my boys, I'm very proud of you. From Monday on you will be „Sextaner", that means your first class in high school is called Sexta. Study hard because next year you will get into Quinta and usually quite a few do not make it. This is your year to show them that you are capable of an academic life." Her eyes were slightly moist as she shook our hands and said goodbye. We were dismissed.

From then on, school took over. I adjusted quickly but it was a lot of work. Six different classes a day each one forty minutes with a fifteen-minute interval. Then home for lunch and homework. On the six subjects that took a great deal of the afternoon.

Because I was so busy I did not notice the change in climate between my parents. One day, however, Mother had combined our upstairs sitting room into a combined dining and living and made the former dining room into a bedroom for herself. Downstairs were a big living room, Father's bedroom, my bedroom, a little entrance hall and a full bath. Upstairs was a kitchen, the new living / dining room, Mother's bedroom and bath, and Annie slept under the roof where a small room had been built for her because the other rooms had been destroyed. We were now living in two separate apartments. Alas, in one house. The change had taken part while our class was on a bike trip in the Rhine over a long weekend. First the reason was Father's snoring that had been annoying Mother. They must have still thought of me as their little boy. Still they entertained a lot at home and went out to see their friends. One time I met the English colonel who invited father to his own hunt but gave him a rifle which was originally Father's and allowed him to join his hunting parties. The rifle had to be returned after the shooting. But Colonel Smith was fair. I'm sure he had stretched the rules to invite a German civilian. Afterwards he also gave Father rabbits, hare and a pheasant or two. All greatly welcomed at home. However, to this day I can't stand rabbit, hare or pheasant. I had my share of that in those meagre years after the war.

I shared my mother's room upstairs because mine was packed with all the excess furniture to make space for the guest in the living room. After the lights were out, I heard her crying.

„Mother, tell me, what's going on?" I said in the dark. Just a little light coming into the room from the street lamp outside inn front of the house. It took her a while to control her sobbing.

„It's finished between Father and I", she said.

„But why? Are you both not happy to be together again after all that time?" I asked.

„I thought we would", she sobbed. „But he has another woman. They met during the war in Mr. Glotz' house.

Suddenly I got Goosebumps. I knew who she was. „Mrs. Greff" I whispered.

„Yes, Mrs. Gudrun Greff, twenty-two years younger than Father and I." She cried again, I took her into my arms.

„Maybe not that we're back, things will change", I tried to comfort her. „Besides, she's married."

„She is a widow. Her husband was killed in action. They were married for only two years", she sobbed.

„How do you know all this is true?" I asked knowing instinctively that it was true.

„Uncle Joe told Aunt Ellie", she said.

Yes, of course, Uncle Joe was in Düsseldorf also during the war. He would know it all. A new emotion was rising in me. Something I had never known before. It was ugly but it was there, and it was called hate. It was a different and difficult emotion to deal with and even more difficult to conceal. I would find that out later. It changed my character considerably because hate has so many allied like cheating, lying, and disobeying. It's a long chain. I saw Father only for lunch, which was never a long affair in our house. Sleeping downstairs, I often heard him enter the house, me being a very light sleeper. It was usually 2 a.m. in the morning. Then news came that Father's mother was ill and could not manage anymore by herself. I had not seen her in years. She lived four hours away by car in a little town. Dad took a factory truck and loaded her and her few belongings up. He put her bed on the truck with her in it and drove her to our house. Mother was never consulted except for the fact that Annie had to vacate her room and sleep on the sofa in the upstairs living / dining room. Grandma's room was then freshly painted. Mother hung some curtains; a rug was put down and some flowers on the windowsill. It was all done very quickly. You could still smell the paint when she arrived. Grandma was seventy-five years old. I was her only grandchild. Although she had four sons. Two were killed in World War I. Peter, my uncle, lived outside of Düsseldorf but he was the black sheep and not much talked about. He was married but had no children. Father was the youngest of the four and had succeeded with Uncle Joe at a brilliant career in machinery. After a week of good nursing by Annie and Mother, Grandma got on her feet again. She just looked like in recent photos. Tiny, only five feet four, but too heavy for her height. Her hair was grey and even curlier than Father's or mine. We all, except Father, helped her to furnish her room as cheerfully as possible. The last carton Grandma emptied herself. There must have been at least fifteen framed photos of me, which she had put around the room.

„Now that I finally have the original, I don't need them actually", she said to nobody in particular. „But I'm so used to them and now he is my boy. But you see, Ada", she looked at her daughter-in-law, „I have him here, only just one month old. A real Jaqulay, is that not so?"

She had a south room and looked into the garden, which interested her more than the house. „Ada'chen" - a diminutive - „when I'm a little better, maybe next week, would you mind if I potter around down there?"

„Do as you like, Grandmother", Mother said. She called her Grandmother just like I did. It did not bother her in the least. I had to remember that although these women had not seen each other during the war, they knew each other for many years when Grandma still lived in Düsseldorf and ran her tobacco shop to feed her four sons. Her husband had died at the age of thirty-eight and Father and Mother knew each other since they were twelve years old. They all came from the same neighbourhood. Including Uncle Joe and Aunt Ellie. It was I who had to get to know my grandmother. While she was still not well, Annie would take her meals upstairs. But sure enough, a week later the old lady was in the garden and she knew what she was doing having lived in the country for twenty years. Grandma and Mother got along just fine. They liked each other I could tell. Father and she were cordial but there was no affection that I could detect. One day I heard her say, „Ada'chen, connect me with Peter please. I want to visit him and take Peter'chen along."

Mother dialled, and Erna, her daughter-in-law, answered the phone. After a brief „hello, and how are you", Grandmother asked to speak to her son. Suddenly she was more relaxed, even joked with my uncle and they made a date for next Sunday including me.

„Ada'chen, Martin does not necessarily have to know we're visiting. Besides, he's never here on Sundays anyhow", she said patting Mother's cheek. That Sunday before we left, Grandma had cut some flowers in the garden and pressed them into my hand.

„For Erna", she stated. We took the tram and changed into a different one and again into a different one. Then after a short walk, I saw a narrow row of houses with a tiny garden in front that was in dying need of Grandma's skills. It was an ugly street with ugly houses. We were expected for four o'clock coffee. Grandma rang, it took a while and Erna opened the door.

„Hello, you're here already. Well, I guess it must be four o'clock then." She giggled in a loud high-pitched voice. I delivered the flowers since I stood in front of Grandma and shook her hand, so did Grandma. We went inside.

„What have you done to your hair, Erna? It's so red." Grandma asked in surprise.

„Oh, you know", she giggled again. She was plump with a kind, very round face and a mop of red hair. It could have been a dress she wore but it looked to me like a short kimono and then I noticed she wore black satin pants with house slippers that had seen better days. In a way she was a mess.

„I bet you don't know me anymore, Peter. You were so small when I saw you last", she giggled again. I put the flowers on the console table.

„Come into the living room", she said. „Your uncle just can't wait to see you. You'll be thirteen soon. Oh yes, he told me", she said. „Please sit in the sofa, Mrs. Jaqulay with Peter. I'll make the coffee."

We looked around that messy room they called the living room. Our eyes met. We were thinking alike. Grandmother got that stern pinched expression around her mouth. The side door was opened and we heard some men laughing.

„No, leave the shit house door open. I have another joke for you, sweethearts." It was my uncle's voice.

Grandmother sat bolt upright and poked her elbows into my ribs.

„Go, close the door immediately", she said. I got up and

closed it but I saw my uncle on the toilet, door open and two young men, sixteen or so, ready for his next joke. They all had beer bottles in their hands. I had just returned to the sofa next to Grandmother when Erna came back.

„What, no Peter yet?" she asked.

She made for the same door I had just closed but she closed it quickly behind her. I carefully glanced through the curtains and saw the two young men make a hasty retreat through the backyard. Grandma had not said a word. The door opened, and Uncle Peter came in straightening his tie.

„Dear mama", he took her into his arms and kissed her left and right „Finally in our home. I've been waiting for so long."

Grandmother took his head into her hands. Tears were running down her old face, she kissed him on the forehead.

„Peter, my son", that was all she said before sitting down again. „Well", cried Peter, „and this is my nephew. Isn't he a beautiful young gentlemen." Standing up, he took me in his arms and planted a wet kiss on my cheek. I would not have minded so much but he reeked of liquor. He held me at arm length.

„You truly look like a Jaqulay. Just like Martin at that age. Curly hair from his Grandma", he laughed good-naturedly. I liked him even though he was slightly tipsy. He was taller than all of us, and slender as a rail. His hair was straight; his eyes were brown-green like mine with a devilish look in them.

„Well, Mama, please excuse us, we had a party last night and it got very late", he said, putting on the charm to modify Grandma who to my surprise fell for it and relaxed.

„Just a second, Mama. Erna, where is the cake?" he asked his wife.

„Oh, goodness, I forgot it completely", she giggled again. „Oh, Peter, it's just at the corner, but I can't go like this", she pleaded.

„I'll go", I said. „We passed the bakery, I know where it is."

„Isn't he a sweetheart", Uncle Peter declared.

Jesus, I wished he wouldn't call me that.

„Just a second, I'll give you the money", he fumbled in his trouser pockets and pulled both linings and said with a sad face, „Sorry, your uncle is penniless again." I saw Grandmother reaching for her purse.

„Never mind, I have the money", I called back running out of the house. So that's how the other side of Father's family lived. There were stories I did not know of yet. That was clear enough. We were four people, so I bought eight pieces of various cakes. Going back I saw the two boys at the corner, still with their beer bottles. One whistled and the other winked at me wickedly. I pretended not to notice. On arriving back, both, mother and son were in a deep conversation. I gave the cakes to Erna in the kitchen. She gave me a tray with milk and sugar on it which I took into the living room. Plates, cups, etc. were on the table already. Their conversation stopped. Erna brought in the cake and then got the coffeepot.

„First comes Mrs. Jaqulay", she spoke to Grandma as she poured hot water in her cup. My uncle sprang up.

„You dumb cow, you forgot to put the coffee in the pot! Give that to me." He grabbed the pot and stormed into the kitchen. Erna glided into the chair and lit a cigarette.

„Oh, this is not my day. Too much schnapps last night, I guess", looking at the ceiling and blowing smoke upwards. Grandma glared at her. I had never seen her so furious, as a matter of fact, she looked like Father after the fruit cake disaster. Finally, we had coffee and cake and not much was spoken.

Then, Uncle Peter said to me, „Peter, come into the yard, I want to show you where I work. „

Behind the house, at the end stood a shack. We went inside and he put some lights on and there stood one large machine just like in our factory. Uncle Peter started it and showed me how he hollowed out round steel into cylinders. In a corner stood a doyen of them ready polished inside and out.

„Those go to the factory tomorrow", he told me. Well, one mystery was solved. Uncle Peter worked for Father in a small capacity. It was clear; the expensive machinery also belonged to Father. The black sheep had been found out. Afterwards, we said goodbye. Before we went around the corner, I saw Uncle Peter standing at the door, a handkerchief quickly appeared from his trousers, he waved and I waved back. Grandmother did not say anything. Neither did I. On the last tram for home she said, „Peter'chen, promise me not to talk about this visit, neither with your father or mother." I promised. It had been a very interesting Sunday.

Annie always had her meals with us. She was not a maid in the usual sense. More of a family member who gave Mother a hand in the house. We did have a cleaning lady besides her who came twice a week. But the unpleasantness between Father and Mother was often too embarrassing, and Annie who knew what was going on agreed upon Mother's request to eat in the kitchen. But that was not good enough for Father. One day he said, „Annie, I want my mother served dinner upstairs. Old ladies have an odour I can't stand. Besides, the steps are too much for her."

We were both stunned. Mother cried, „It's your mother, you tell her yourself, you coward."

But Grandmother who was about to come in had heard. She entered the dining room.

„That will not be necessary. I have heard Martin. If you do

not want me at your table, I'll eat upstairs. It's your house, after all."

With that, she turned, slammed the door. And I heard her go upstairs. I started to cry. Father threw his napkin down and left his meal unfinished. The whole thing was a nightmare. I hated Father even more for that cruelty. From that day on, Grandmother never ate a meal with us. Mother's nerves were shot. Barely was there a day she did not cry and barely a lunch without them shouting at each other.

My Confirmation was going to be a big event. My first real suit with long pants, black shoes, white shirt and tie. I was very proud. The exam in church had gone fine. I was asked three questions and knew the answers. Aunts and uncles came, cousins, Uncle Joe and Aunt Ellie, and Lisa. But Father had organised it all. It must have cost al lot of money because it was all black market. The whole affair was spoiled for me because Father was not there at the party. He was off somewhere with Mrs. Greff. By then, everybody knew he had a mistress. He was unfortunately not a discreet man and was seen with her all over town. Shortly after the Confirmation, the German Deutsch Mark was established. Things changed quickly economically for all of us. But not within the family. Grandmother announced one day she was going to the cemetery. The grave of her second son was being moved to another place. His name had been Carl. He had died of gas poisoning during World War I and was in an airtight casket with a window over his face. Before transfer of his casket, Grandmother wanted to see her son once more. She offered for us to come along, but no one was willing. So she went by herself. „Just as I remembered him", she said upon her return. „My son is asleep."

I sat often with Grandmother. She was a good storyteller. Even spoke a little French which she taught me. After her arrival in Düsseldorf many years ago, and before she married, she was a maid in the house of a famous actress born as French-German and managed our legitimate theatre in town. My grandfather was born in Belgium, and all his ancestors were French. That's why I have a French name.

In the fall, she got pneumonia and never recovered. I saw her daily several times. Often she called for Peter. Not for me, but for her son. Then she went into a coma. We kept all the doors open to hear her heavy breathing, and then suddenly it stopped. I raced up the stairs. Grandmother was dead, and I closed her eyes softly. Her funeral was small. Uncle Peter came without Erna. My father did not attend.

I remember it was a hot day. I was alone in the house and reading a romantic novel that actually belonged to Mother. Suddenly, I remembered Kasper in the hospital. I got undressed and studied myself in the mirror. Slowly, I let my hands glide over my body. It felt exciting. I lay down on my bed and started to masturbate. It took a while until slowly I felt that most wonderful sensation that Kasper had told me about. It was wonderful and disturbing at the same time. A while later I tried it again. I closed my eyes and started to fantasise. All I saw was Kaspar, my schoolmates and our sport instructor who had taken us to the pool for swimming lessons and whose big bulge in his very brief bathing suit I had noticed. I did not use my bike for school anymore but had a pass for the Tram. The station was only a short walk from school. At lunchtime it was always terribly overcrowded. Passengers stood like in a sardine can. On several occasions I would feel a hand of a stranger casually pressing against my leg and ever so casually travelling towards my crotch. I always pretended not to notice but it was terribly exciting and I always got a hard on right away. Across the platform was a large newspaper stand and public facilities underneath. One day I had to go, although I hated the smell.

It was almost empty but then a man stood next to me and started to play with himself until he achieved an enormous erection. I stared in fascination and also got a hard on which seemed to please him because he smiled and winked at me. Quickly I made an exit and ran for the next tram. I was shaking with excitement and could not wait to get home and lock myself into the bathroom to masturbate.

One evening, I believe Mother and Annie had gone to the movies, I took the tram into town to the newspaper stand. I saw him leaning against the railing, pretending to read a newspaper, but actually watching the men enter the facilities. He spotted me, rolled up his paper and smiled. Then he slowly walked to a little park nearby. I followed at a distance but he knew I was following. In a very dark corner he sat down on a bench. I sat next to him and not a word was spoken. He opened his fly and took out his tool. He took my hand and I touched it. Slowly he made my hand move. He got erect very quickly and I masturbated his great dick until he came. Then he opened my fly, knelt down between my legs and started fellatio. I came within seconds. He got up, playfully tapped my head with his newspaper and disappeared in the dark. I got home before the movie ended and pretended to be asleep when I heard the front door open.

After the house was quiet, I lay awake for a long time. My head was spinning. It had been great, but also dangerous and it was wrong. Indecent jokes were told in class and they always concerned girls of course. Masturbation was never mentioned, however. I liked girls a lot and they liked me, but they never made me think of sex. All my fantasies centred around men. There was something very wrong I knew. There was something Kasper had not told me about. Next day I bought a newspaper and found in the advertisement section offered a book on sex. It was promised to be sent discretely in just plain brown paper. I cut out the ad, ordered it and paid at the Post Office. In those days we got mail twice a day. It was all very tricky but luck was on my side, it arrived a few days later in the afternoon mail. First it told me everything I knew already. But then came chapters about abnormal sex. There it was all in print and very precisely so. The symptoms were all there; overprotective Mother, Father never home, few kids of my age to play with. More interested in things female than male. The great attraction was a homosexual, a criminal even, an outcast of society. Somebody perverse, the focus of awful jokes and names. Worst of all, nobody to talk to - absolutely nobody. I was a living disgrace, should anybody ever find out.

I took it all very hard, lost several pounds and looked pale and awful. My parents noticed and sent me to a Doctor who prescribed this and that, I threw it all away. I knew he could not help me. My marks in school started to sink alarmingly. Then Father had one of his great ideas. I had to take piano lessons. He bought a black monster which crammed my room and I hated it. Only the best teacher would do of course. He expected me to be a virtuoso within the year. My first teacher was a lady, a truly great musician. And even though Father paid well, after a month she delegated me to one of her male pupils.

Mr. Hernhard was an eyeful! Tall, young, long brunette hair that was supposed to be the sign of an artist. His eyes were large and grey, so was his suit. When he sat next to me at the piano I could see his masculine legs through the pants. He was clean and smelled fresh and was ever so business-like with his little pupil. I thought he was wonderful, maybe he was 22 or 23. His hands were that of a pianist, strong, long and well manicured. After the lesson he would smoke a cigarette, relax and talk.

„You know, Peter, you will never be a musician. You just don't have it."

„I know, I do it for Father. Christmas is coming and I have to learn a few pieces, it would please him and Mother so much," I said. He was honest, „I have to make money to get me through the conservatory. I will teach you the Christmas Carols but I don't think I will teach you afterwards."

Well, he taught me for two more years but not because I was musical! I could draw and paint rather well, never did I have lessons. After one of our sessions, he smoking his cigarettes, I showed him my album which he liked. I let one leaf drop on the floor and retrieved it between his legs, getting up slowly I casually touched his big crotch and got up between his legs. Our eyes met, I wanted to hand him the sheet, instead he grabbed me and kissed me on the lips. His tongue worked itself into my mouth and I responded eagerly. He paused for a while.

„You'll never be a pianist, Peter, but you are my most beautiful pupil, I adore you." With that he opened his fly and a wonderful long big cock appeared which he started to masturbate. Quickly I was between his legs again and sucked on that gorgeous thing until he came, while he was playing the „Liebestod."

„Now it's your turn," he said.

But I had been so excited, I had come in my pants already.

„Next time Oskar," I said, calling him the first time by his first name.

„You are too good for words," he kissed me again.

„Until next week, you wonderful witch." He laughed and left. I was adored, a new feeling, a new wonderful feeling"! Up to then I had never thought about my physique of face. My parents had always dressed me well and I like my clothes but never had I thought about my appearance much. Compliments to my parents about their cute little boy came back to me. That night, stark naked I had a good look at myself in the mirror from all sides. „Oscar is right" I thought, „your are a pretty witch." I examined my face closely. Curly brown hair, lots of it. Big brown and green eye-brows, a little red mouth, nicely shaped, the lower lip a little larger. And the skin a little pale maybe, but absolutely flawless. The high forehead, did they not say that was a sign of intelligence? The body was too skinny yet, but the legs were muscular if not too long. Well my dick was not fully grown and I could not yet fold the foreskin over like Oskar or the man in the park. But the buns were all there, strong and round and not too big, like two bowling balls. I wondered why they all playfully hit my rear-end? „Well," I thought, „with a little exercise we will get those pectorals working!" The nipples stood straight out. The following day Oscar dared to call home but I was alone at the house. Would I like to come and visit him at five p.m. in his flat? Yes I would and yes I went. What an afternoon, what a physique, what a lover, what excitement.

After it was all over, Oskar had quit on me suddenly - no explanation, and I felt lonely. I knew there were options but I did not persue any of them. One day we got out of the blue a new boy in our class. He was seated in front of me. The boys were curious of course and so was I. He had come from a village quite a few miles away, but his folks lived near Düsseldorf. His name was Olaf, my age, but he was a giant compared to me. First he intimidated me but after a brief talk during classes, I found out that his family and mine knew each other through the business.

Olaf was very handsome at sixteen. Brown hair and hazel eyes, high cheekbones and a figure of an athlete. He soon was our goal keeper in the football team. Unfortunately, I had to play football too and hated every minute of it. Talking to Olaf, however, was a completely different thing altogether.

He was quietly spoken, not the rough goal keeper you would expect. He was extremely intelligent. Maybe my family could cut more mustard in town than his, anyhow, I felt he liked to talk to me more than to the other guys. That was noticed by the class in which I had many friends. However, he was the new one, he had to be tested, which Olaf did with bravura playing football. A few weeks later he was „in" with the other guys.

Mostly, the talk was about their and our business. He knew I was a lazy football player and was more interested in the arts, but so was he, besides sports. We took the same tram after school for some of the way, he had to get off earlier than I.

One day, a classmate who I was very fond of asked me point blank, „You and Olaf seem to have kicked it off quite nicely?"

I knew that all of the class was behind him!

„It's none of your business," I retorted, „he's a nice fellow and our goal keeper." That shut him up. But there was a special incident.

The boy to my right, Detlef, never liked me and vice versa. Right from „Sexta" on. He always tried to pick a fight with me but now it seemed he was boiling because of the casual friendship between Olaf and I.

One day I wore white tennis sneakers to class. In those days a novelty. Before class, Detlef noticed them and made fun of me. „They wear them in the U.S.A. all the time" I told him. Nose up, he replied, „We are not in the U.S.A."

The ground was wet, he dipped me into a puddle, and royally ruined my white sneakers. The class was laughing at me. I hit him, although he was stronger than I was. He hit back and before long, we were battling in the puddle. Then out of nowhere appeared big Olaf, he got us two apart and smashed Detlef to a pulp - before class - and in front of all the boys - Detlef was bleeding and fled to the boys room, while Olaf yelled at all of them, „Should any of you ever put a finger on Peter, I'll kill him!"

Dead silence, class was called and we went in. From that moment, I had my hero. Later I thanked Olaf, after I had cleaned myself. Detlef and I were late for class by a few minutes! School then was from 8 p.m. to 12 p.m., then home for lunch (the big meal in Germany) then homework for at least until 4 p.m. One day, after class, I got a call from Olaf.

„Would I like to go with him to the movies? Esther Williams in Bathing Beauty"

I almost fell to the floor. Would I? With that hunk, my protector of course I would - and we went! Good taste always prevails, he had bought us tickets in the „Loge" and we had the box to ourselves. An American movie, what a thrill, and Esther spoke German fluently. What fun!

I joined, if not actively, all the clubs he belonged to. It did not make any difference to me. Everything was just window-dressing, as long as he was with me, and he always was.

But, and there always is a „but" in everybody's life, he never told me that he loved „me".

One winter, he took a vacation skiing in Bavaria. I went with mother, having Olaf on my arm all the time. When we met on our special Tuesday, he told me about this lovely girl he had fallen in love with. He went on and on, I was falling, falling - was it over?

I was numb, that girl had won, I was hurt, my pride was level zero. Four years later, he falls in love with a girl - and where am I - I love you Olaf, you have been my life for four years, what am I to do?

„Olaf, be happy with your girl." I took him by the arm and walked him out of the house.

I felt drained, empty inside. I lost interest in absolutely everything. Even my parents noticed the change in my attitude to life, but naive as they were they never could figure out the reason why their son looked ill and was so detached from everybody.

„Why does Olaf not come to visit anymore?" Mother asked one day. „Did you have a fight? A fall out? What has happened?" she wanted to know.

„Mother, we are now of a certain age, Olaf and I. The close camaraderie is over, he found a girl. She is now all that he has on his mind. I am not important to him anymore, understand?"

„Well, that will happen, but no reason to cancel an old friendship" she replied.

„When father met me and uncle Jack and Aunt Ellie, well we were all the best of friends you know, and later even married."

„I know all that mother, but I do not have a steady girl like Olaf, I feel left out," I lied.

„Well, then it's about time you met one" she said. „And the best way is to enrol you into a social dancing class. Aunt Ellie has been after me for a while already. You should go to class with Lisa. You will meet lots of girls there, you'll see. Shall I set it up for you?"

What was the use, she would never understand my problem and so Lisa and I were enrolled into the finest social dancing class in town.

Of course, by renomé we were accepted eagerly. The trouble was, however, all the other boys were two years older than I and Lisa had blossomed to rather ample proportions. But of course to have the „Juniors" of a well known factory as their pupils, the „Königs" were delighted to have us, it was a good feather in their cap.

Anyhow, the boys either felt sorry for me, or my preciousness made up for it, or maybe they just felt sorry for that skinny boy to dance all the time with that heavy girl. But we were left alone, and there were no ugly comments. To be fair, I must admit we all got along just fine and I relaxed.

Lisa was very light on her feet. She had one of the prettiest faces amongst the other girls and naturally was the best dressed, and a very fast learner. Thank God, Olaf was not there, I do not think otherwise I could have gone through with it all. But the other girls, some I knew from the clubs, were there. They, of course, were greatly amused that Peter and Lisa were in their class. Well, we must have been the odd couple, and whenever there was „Damenwahl", the girls asked the boys to dance. I had two or three of them to ask me. Puppi, my favourite, an excellent dancer, said, „Don't get a big head because three of us ask you to dance with us, but we actually feel sorry for you that you have to train with that fat Lisa". Now was that not a sweet consolation I ask you? Mr. König, the dance master, looked like a retired gigolo from old Berlin. He taught the girls. His wife, Carmelitta König was probably ten years older than him and must have fallen into a paint box before every lesson. Never, ever have I seen so much make-up on a woman's face, and all wrongly put on. Nevertheless, she was slim and very gracious. Because, besides the steps of all the dances from a Waltz throughout to Paso Doble, she also told us etiquette! For me, it was hilarious, having been brought up in a hotel, but the others had to learn. How to seat a lady, what to do with a napkin, how to cross your legs, not to re-arrange your hair at a table and so on and so forth.

Then came the middle Ball (after six month) held in the golden „Saal" on the Rhine. With parents of course viewing what their offspring's had learned. Everybody was dressed up. The boys in their first dinner jackets, the girls in evening gowns. Lisa wore a lovely gown in black taffeta, her blond hair swept up, she was quite a lady.

Naturally, we were all nervous because the parents were present. The affair went of very smoothly.

Six months later came the final ball, this time winners were picked, a terrible affair for us students. Lisa however, cool and realistic, knew that Puppi and I made a better team. Since we were selected for the winning group, six couples only, she consented gracefully. Puppi was in a steel blue taffeta. Slender and much tinier than I, the proportions were right. We had trained, privately for hours on end. Finally, the six couples were on, in various dances. Unfortunately, Puppi had forgotten before the waltz to make a deep curtsey in front of me, but I know, nobody had told us before to do so. Even so, we were the most popular pair on the floor from Rumba to Tango, but that fatal mistake at the waltz got us only the second prize. Well, we thought, better than no prize at all! Many years later when we waltzed at Olaf's silver wedding, she curtsied and I bowed before we waltzed, nobody else did it of course, it was our „In" joke. Never to be forgotten.

After the Gymnasium, and after the dancing classes, I was informed by my father that he had decided to put me to work in the factory as an apprentice for a year, since their competition had refused to take me. It apparently was not a question of what profession I wanted to go into. He had decided that his only son would follow in his foot-steps and learn the business from scratch, just like him when he was a youngster. Start at the bottom and get to know it all, marry Lisa later and the money and the factory would all stay in one pot. Make many sons and we will live happily ever after, and then the two of them could retire in peace, as simple as that.

I was seventeen years old then and had ideas for costume design, as well as stage design or even becoming an actor. Anything in the arts - but not a manufacturer of machinery. „Look at your friend Olaf, he will sometimes take over his fathers business," he told me.

Yes, Olaf could, and wanted to do that, but not I. But fathers word was the law and I found myself in blue overalls in the machinery hall, ruling away at a piece of metal with my manicured fingernails.

I hated it all, the noise, the smells, the dirt. Most of all when father came with that evil grin to watch me making a fool of myself. Then I learned to blot things completely out of my mind. I did what I was told to do, but my mind was wandering in quite different directions.

Lunch was at home, without me changing out of the overalls, because it was only one hour and then back to the factory. The marriage between my parents was finished by then. Lunch was glum, they fought constantly and I was the silent participant. Three unhappy people at one table, except maybe father looking forward to meeting Mrs. Greff. My fellow workers treated me like I had leprosy. I was the son of the boss, naturally I was the spy planted amongst them to report to the old man. They were not happy with me around and neither was I. I was sent from station to station. Always new faces, always new machines to teach me various machinery's. At the electric drill, my fault, I had not secured the drill tight enough with the key into the machine. Putting the iron piece under it, the drill slipped out and hurt my hand rather badly. I screamed and there was a lot of blood. Well, it was an accident that happens daily in factories.

Suddenly ten people were there to help me. Took me to the infirmary and had my hand bandaged, all of them suddenly helpful and concerned. Father made light of it, after he was sure that the accident was not all that bad.

Bandaged, I was back the following day, drilling along as best I could. The frosty spell with the workmen was broken from then on and slowly I became one of them. That had only taken six long months of misery. Things changed rapidly. I did not go home for lunch anymore, not much was lost there anyhow, but I ate with them, bringing my lunch in a „Henkelmann" like they did. We slowly got friendly. They understood that the competition would not have me and that I had to learn at fathers factory. Also, that I was not spying on them and telling tales to the Boss. Then came the dirty jokes, well I had a few of my own also, which they hat not expected from the Bosses son. Some of the younger workers were very handsome. Big muscular arms and the riskier the jokes, the more the overalls bulged. I had two favourites. Today they would be in the magazines, but I had to be ever so careful and made up stories about the girls I screwed, which they ate up. As much as I hated my fathers plans to make me a manufacturer in his firm, it was finally a good feeling that the personnel accepted me completely, and since we were all per „Du", that Peter would eventually become their Boss.

Herta Noel was a stunning looking lady. She was a singer with a lovely contralto voice. She had met Mr. Glotz through Mrs. Greff. But times were bad and she had had no engagements for some time. She finally became a house-keeper for a short time to Mr. Glotz. As careless as he was with his belongings, she stole a ring from one of his numerous jewel boxes, things he would present to his paramours time and time again. Glotz did not press charges but dismissed her. Mrs. Greff, who Glotz adored, knew the story. Besides, Noel had borrowed a considerable amount of money from her. Father knew nothing about it and engaged her to sing and entertain at his 50th Birthday Party. Mr. Glotz was a very ill man. He had been treated for his heart for a long time. He was obese and drank far too much. Mrs. Greff disliked his advances enormously, knowing too well that father loved her, besides, father was much richer than Mr. Glotz. Before the party, to which Mrs. Greff could not be invited for obvious reasons, she called Herta to meet in a coffee house.

„Herta, you know how ill Glotz is, now that damn party at the Jacoulay's, you will be there! You know how Glotz hates to take his medicine. Now, you watch over him and if he feels ill, please put this powder into his glass.“

With that, she handed her a small package, like a commercial restaurant sugar bag. Herta promised to take care of Mr. Glotz!

One year after the German Deutsch Mark, father celebrated his fiftieth birthday. It was going to be a private party in our house, in the big living room. Almost all the furniture was cleared away, except for the „L“-shaped banquet and the chairs of which many more had to be added, the famous folding ballroom variety. An enormous table was create by our talented carpenters from the factory. We had to accommodate fifty people. My bedroom looked like a warehouse and that night I slept upstairs in mothers room. The small entrance hall had a round table and chairs for the artists that were to perform that evening. Father made it into a stag party, with Mother the only lady. The reason was obvious because Gudrun could not be present. Invited were the gentlemen of the Düsseldorf Industries, his bowling cronies, who overlapped into Industry, and all the higher staff from the factory. Naturally Mr. Glotz and some of his friends from the Art Gallery. Everybody knew everybody, introductions were superfluous. The entire staff from „Bar Charlotte“ was in attendance, and food and drink also catered for by that place. Three musicians from „Bar Charlotte“ were included. The main artist, a tenor from the Opera, was a friend who later made it to Bayreuth and the Met in New York. The female singer was Herta Noel, equally well known by this crowd. The youngest and loveliest entertainer came from our legitimate Theatre, but she was very versatile and could sing and dance. Later, she also became a famous actress both on stage and television. After a long dinner, the entertainment began. Half of the table was cleared and turned into a stage. I had to announce the artists and father wanted me to perform with two of my best Marionettes. Naturally, the applause for Junior was built in, I felt terribly embarrassed that father showed me off. The tenor was the big star, known by everybody from the Opera House, he sang lovely arias and also folk songs. The little young actress used the bathroom to change and emerged as an Hawaiian Hoola Dancer to the delight of all those lecherous men.

After that, Herta Noel entertained father's guests with popular songs of the time. The party was a smash success and no party in later years could compare with that one. Enormous amounts of liquor were consumed, speeches galore, communal singing and „schunkeln".

Mr. Glotz had a ball, with the Hoola-girl next to him. Suddenly he turned white, threw up over the table and put his head akimbo in all that mess. The girl tried to give him a glass of water, but he refused. The waiters cleaned up immediately. Not many in the group had noticed that he was ill but Herta Noel screamed!

„It's probably one of his attacks!" She fumbled for her purse, got a glass of water and from the small envelope, put the contents into the glass. She lifted his head, „Here sugar, Mama always takes care of you." Glotz responded to her and drank slowly, „Thank you my dear" he mumbled. The colour returned to his face and he grinned. The friends around him who had noticed, roared with laughter. „Drunk again, what else is new", was their comment.

A few minutes later Glotz collapsed again. This time father was alert and made his way to the phone in the ball and called an ambulance. The two girls managed to get him out of the smoke filled room, father opened the front door. The fresh air seemed to help him. „Sorry old chap, great party, and such lovely nurses", he said. The ambulance was there, Glotz was put on a stretcher and off he went to the hospital. Upon arrival he was dead.

Olaf was my best friend for many years. Never did he know about my proclivity until many years later, when he had married a lovely lady. Then it did not matter to him or to her. We are still very good friends.

After we left the gymnasium (college) he worked in his father's factory and I in mine, but we never lost contact - sometimes I think even his lovely lady knew that there was a very strong bond between us, which in her wisdom she never tried to interrupt!

And then I was sent off to England! The war was nine years over, I was twenty years old. The idea came from father of course, who wanted to cut me off Mother's apron-strings. Through his banking connections he had procured for me a voluntary job in a Swiss Bank in London. That meant no salary (he sent me the money to live on but even in 1954 a City like London was much more expensive than Düsseldorf).

During the time working in the factory, I had taken more English lessons with a delightful old lady who had worked before the war at the London Times. Therefore, her accent was far superior to our gymnasium teacher. My train was to leave Düsseldorf at 2 p.m. Sleeping compartment to Ostende, then ferry, another train into Victoria Station.

My friends from the dancing school picked me up at the house which was a big surprise and drove me to the station. It was not a long drive but a very liquid one, they had seen to that. I was very touched and realised how popular I actually was and that they were genuinely sad to see me go.

The train came from Munich, my companion in the lower berth was snoring. I climbed up as carefully as possible.

In Ostende the whole train was put onto the ferry. Finally, the „White Cliffs of Dover". It's like the Loreley on the Rhine, once was enough!

At 4 p.m. finally Victoria Station. I needed a porter and a taxi. Of course nobody in Germany had warned me that the English speak with various accents. Well, I got the porter, he found the taxi and loaded my belongings and off we went to the Y.M.C.A. in Tottenham Court Road. This had been a suggestion of my English teacher, since father had not bothered with such details!

This postage-stamp size room was red. Fireman red, including the ceiling. I have nothing against this colour, it comes in lovely shades, but this was too much.

Next morning I lined up for breakfast - what the hell is porridge and kippered herring?! Enough! In a paper I found an address in a Swiss-English Boarding house in Devonshire Terrace. Off I went by cab. It looked ok and the land-lady spoke a little German. I got a room, back view of rows of old brick buildings. The heat cost a shilling to be inserted into a contraption near the fireplace. But the walls were white, what a delight! Bath and facilities were at the end of the corridor. Bathing day for me on Fridays, between 6 p.m. and 7 p.m. Oh, I almost forgot, there was a sink in the room with cold water. But in all honesty the price was right!

I had three days before my job began and started to look around. Unfortunately, I had arrived in November. In those days there was a thing called „smog". I ran into a lot of strangers and did not see much of the city. Alas, I opted for the indoors. Out of the corner pub I noticed, fell one drunk after the other. How was I to know they closed at 11 p.m., but in I went anyway. Not knowing the measures of beer, I pointed to a small glass. So far so good. Before I knew it, I was talked to. It could have been Chinese but turned out to be cockney, which my darling teacher had overlooked.

The peroxide barmaid was helpful. All I wanted was the address of a good Turkish Bath, which she gave me and off I went to the Russel Square bath. The taxi drove me through half of London it seemed, but I got there.

The elevator went at least ten storeys down. First they wanted my new shoes, like in a Mosque, which I carefully relented but got a token for them. Well, here I was in an enormous edifice resembling the interior of Westminster Abbey. The attendants guessing I was a foreigner, or at least a new face, were most helpful. Arriving here definitely was nicer than Victoria Station. I soon found the steam room, you could almost smell it. It was built in three tiers of white marble. „Smog" again, I thought, but this time with naked gentlemen. Once the eyes got accustomed to the very dim light, I could make out the clientele, a lot of them were old and fat. I saw someone on the third tier against the wall. He was young, clean-shaven, and muscular.

„Please sit down, tonight is not my night with all those fat cows," he said.

I sat down, he had a lovely face, besides I could understand his English!

The more my eyes got used to the steam, the more beautiful he looked. Brunette hair, brown eyes, a body to die over. He was very young, not overdeveloped in the muscle structure but definitely someone who worked with his body. He smiled at me with good, gleaming teeth. I smiled back and took my towel off. He looked and seemed to like what he saw and spread his legs. Well, it was all there. Very slowly his head came closer to mine. We looked into each others eyes.

„I would like to kiss you," he said. I nodded, and we kissed.

First the lips touched ever so slightly. Very slowly he put his arm around me, then pressed his mouth harder on mine, until we actually kissed each other. Naturally, our penises were up. „Not here," he said, „I have a room, you come with me if it's ok." Simultaneously we got up. „Meet you in front," he said. I rushed into my clothes and took the elevator upstairs. He was waiting there in his dark blue sailor uniform, cap and all, showing a large bulge in his pants.

I hailed a taxi. He also lived in a boarding house, not far from me. We undressed in seconds. He insisted on anal sex, something new to me. But he was very gentle and experienced, I did not mind it at all. We had a wonderful night of love. At 6 a.m. he was awake.

„Michael" I said, „I have a room too, shall we meet at 1 p.m. at the Serpentine in the park?"

„Yes dear," he said sleepily. He did not see it, but I slipped ten pounds into his sailor jacket. That must have been a mistake, I meant well, sailors got paid, but I think I insulted him. He never showed up at the Serpentine. After all it had been he who propositioned me first in the bath, therefore I was his boy and not supposed to pay him.

When you are a young man living in London on a budget, you learn quickly that taxis are far too expensive, and you must learn the tube system. The London tube is very simple and wonderfully efficient. To go to the City of London, I needed only one line without changing. It was as simple as apple pie, from Queensway to Bank.

I got to my so-called job on a Monday morning, arriving at the bank at 8.50 a.m. It was a huge building, completely shut. At 9.10 somebody opened the gates. I was dressed in a dark grey flannel suit, white shirt, black shoes, and wore a very dark red tie. Again, there was „smog". Slowly the employees trickled into the building. I asked directions to the manager's office. A fat but jolly man welcomed me. He used the internal phone and another man appeared to take me to the office I was to start in. Crossing the main hall, I noticed that the „smog" had managed to get inside. You could barely see from one side to the other. The office, however, was on the second floor. It turned out to be the Commercial Credit Department. The boss of this office was another fat, jolly gentleman. I was put at a large desk, opposite two females. One was very pretty, the other one much less so. She sat opposite me with her carrot red hair and thick spectacles. Her make-up would have been enough for a whole theatre company. We introduced each other, she smiled sweetly, „I am Miss Darling." As it turned out later, she was true to her name and tried to help me a great deal. I could type, although with two fingers only and was supposed to write letters of credit, by her instructions. The typewriter had to have been ca 1900. I was so inhibited because of my bad English that I did not dare to speak for days. The girls talked and I typed away. Next day my boss told me that grey flannel would not do, only a dark blue suit. More embarrassment. I called my father to wire money for the new suit. According to all the approving glances about my new finery, I guessed I had scored.

Miss Darling was delighted. Then I came across a word I did not know. It was relatively quiet in the office when I asked Miss Darling „Would you tell me please, what does beneficiary mean?" She beamed with delight to be of help, because she had learned German in Switzerland.

„Mr. Jaqulay, doos is der Begünstigte" she translated in what she thought was high German.

There was dead silence in the office for a second and then much laughter and clapping. I was confused, when the boss declared, „My God, he can speak English." The ice was broken and my inhibitions too. From then on it was smooth sailing for me. No matter how many mistakes I made, I talked. The English are very polite people, God bless them, they never laughed when I slaughtered their language.

Miss Darling had taken a great fancy towards me, and really tried to get my language problems going. It was a Friday when she asked me „Mr. Jaqulay, my parents live in the country not far from London, it would be ever so nice if you would spend the week-end with us, you would be most welcome."

I very regretfully declined because my German girlfriend was arriving in London that week-end.

„Oh, how very nice for you" she replied icily! I had been a good try on her part. Even though she did not talk to me for the rest of the day, on Monday she had recovered!

There was one reward in my unpaid job - I got luncheon tickets for a certain „Restaurant". That place was as far down as the tube. That is, it rattled a lot. The soup was every day called „Brown Windsor". On Mondays it was like water. On Fridays it was almost like a pudding, you could stick your spoon in without it falling to the rim of the plate. For my 21st birthday I had saved my pennies. My favourite German dance-school partner was in town and I invited her for a supper-dance to the Café de Paris. We had a delightful meal, danced a lot and ate a lot of cold food because we danced too much. I had ordered a bottle of French champagne, which we sipped very slowly, no money for another one.

Half the bottle was empty. We were on the dance floor all dressed to the top, when at midnight the band stopped. Then came the National Anthem. The couples disentangled, stood to attention, ran to the cloak room and disappeared. What could we do but go - a shame for the half bottle of champagne!

Next day at the bank, a rather „dandified" gentleman took me aside. „Last night I was in the Café de Paris on the first tier, I saw you dancing with a very pretty girl. Fancy seeing you there drinking champagne! Your old man must be pretty well oiled."

When my time at the Bank was up, I took the two girls I had worked with for lunch at „Pimms". No more „Windsor" soup. They were flabbergasted and delighted. We lunched on oysters, champagne, roast beef, Yorkshire pudding, trifle etc. It all was so much fun. For my first stay in London they had bought me the Trafalgar Column with Nelson on top, made out of silvery plastic!

Meanwhile, in Germany, after Mr. Glotz was dead, the reason - heart failure, Father bought the property and contents from his sister who flew in from California. Immediately he made Gudrun manager of the new-old gallery. She was an excellent business lady and with father's connections, the gallery flourished immediately. It was in full swing when I returned from England. As book-keeper come saleslady he employed a once rich lady who had to flee to the West from Russian occupation, leaving everything behind except her jewels, which happened to fit into a large Crocodile handbag and she had not forgotten her stone-marters which she actually wore to work in the winter to the great envy of Gudrun.

She once told me „Mr. Jaqulay, never go for the daisies, always for the orchids, don't forget", and I never did.

I was to become international, and now father sent me to France, that is Paris. Naturally I was thrilled, even more to because he had bought me a brand new car with a silvery metallic sheen which was „in" that year.

Poor Mother, of course, did not like the idea. Suffering from Father's affair with Gudrun and the fact that now she managed a gallery paid for by her husband. However, still no word about a divorce. The night before I left, Father gave me a lesson about French whores and homosexuals. I pretended to listen attentively. Poor Father, if he only knew!

The month was June and I was on my way to Paris. This time the allowance was large and I was to work at one of his representatives, who sold amongst other things our hydraulic products. Again, no preparations had been made where I would stay. This time it would be no Y.M.C.A. or a shoddy boarding house for me. A load of information I had gathered about Paris and had opted for an Hotel on the left Bank, right on the Place St. Michael. No highways then, and the trip via Brussels into the country to France was a sheer delight. My room I had reserved by phone and it was everything I expected. High, above the trees, it overlooked to the left the Boulevard St. Michael and to the right the Seine!

My first night I went to the „Bœuf sur le toit", then an intimate gay bar. At the piano was a gorgeous singer who could not take his eyes off me. During his intermission he sat next to me at the bar, even bought me a Coca Cola. He talked a blue streak, only to find out that my French was practically non-existent - but he spoke English. Yves was the typical Parisian artist on the way up. Jet black hair, lovely blue eyes, he could have been Irish. His voice was well suited to chansons, which he delivered with great charm, only the latest and the naughtiest, without imitating any great star of the time. He rented an apartment in Neuilly, and that is where I drove him. Yves was so well endowed it took a while to get him erect. He also had a patroness, who was a divorce, probably well of, who ran her own hat salon for ladies. If they had an affair I never found out, but after one stormy week with me, it did not matter anymore, because of another gentleman I met. My job was so boring, because of my lack of French, I sat at an adding machine. After one week I suggested to Father's sales agent that I should be in the office from 9 a.m. to 12 p.m. and then go to the Alliance Francaise on the Boulevard Raspail and take French lessons. He agreed and why not, he did not have to pay me a salary. The French class started at 3 p.m. so that I had three hours to spare. It was a beautiful summer and I spent these hours in the Piscine Delighny, a pool with all facilities, anchored to the Seine, near the Boulevard St. Germain. In my new, white bikini, I put down my large towel next to an even larger red one, which was unoccupied at the time. Obviously the occupants were changing or in the pool, or had lunch. After a while, two gents sat down, coming from the pool. The older could have been well into his fifties, the other one in his twenties. Through my sunglasses I studied them, trying not to be too obvious. I turned onto my stomach to ogle them better.

The older guy fell almost immediately asleep, once he hit the blanket. The younger one pretended to read a newspaper, glancing at me once in a while. His hair was blond, he had a great, tanned body. When he took off his glasses, I saw big blue eyes. He smiled at me, I smiled back, lowering my glasses. „By any chance, are you from Cleveland?" he asked me. „No", I said, controlling a laugh, „I am from Deutschland".

I thought „Well, anything will do to open a conversation" and I asked him „and where are you from?"

„I am American" he said, a proud ring to his voice.

That summer, Paris was packed with Americans. The almighty Dollar bought them about everything.

„I work here in a show, I am a singer", he added.

„I try to learn French", looking at my watch, „I have to be off soon to the Alliance Francaise", I said.

„My name is Fred", he said, extending his hand.

„And mine is Peter", as we shook hands. He gave me the name of the Club he worked in.

„It's near Place Pigalle" he said, „I would like very much to meet you again, Peter, how about tomorrow night? It's the fourth of July", he said.

Looking at the other guy, I whispered „Is that your boyfriend?"

„You don't have to whisper, he speaks only French", and then, „No, he is not my boyfriend, we work in the same show".

Yes, I wanted to meet that Fred again. „Ok then, tomorrow night at the „Fiaker", I said, „do you know the place?"

„But of course", he replied, „I'll be late, however, my last show finishes at 2a.m."

Before Yves and I had parted, he rented me his small apartment in Neuilly. It was much cheaper than the hotel. He wanted to spend the summer in Cannes and needed the money to travel. He explained the situation to the concierge and I paid him three months in advance. It was a modern building, very clean, and had an elevator. I felt very happy to have my own flat, as small as it was.

The day I met Fred, concentration in school was zero and I was glad when it was over. I drove up the Champs-Elysée to the Etoile and off to Neuilly. After a long nap, I decided to find the Club in which Fred worked, and see the show.

Parking was never easy in Paris, finally I found a spot on the Place Pigalle. All those neon lights turned the night to day - and so many Clubs. I asked several doormen and found „La Nouvelle Eve". Fred's photo was in the window - I was there. At the box office I got a ticket for the Bar, which included a glass of champagne. When I entered, the show was in progress. But wow - what elegance, what glamour, the eyes could not take it in all at once. The large room was built in a circle, so was the stage, which was lit from underneath. The orchestra sat stage left and tables around the stage in two tiers. From the bar, I had an excellent view over that lovely Club. The air was filled with the various perfumes of the ladies. Many men wore tuxedoes, but in my dark blue suit I felt quite comfortable. A girl came to the bar and I bought a souvenir album, when Fred Douglas was announced. There he was, in smart black pants and white short jacket and black bow tie. His beautiful voice filled the room. From stage left and right, staircases were lowered and the girls descended like feathers, all in sky blue chiffon, wearing enormous hats in the same colour made out of ostrich plumes. The program read „All costumed designed by Pierre Balmain".

It was a breathtaking sight, the girls circling the stage, showing off their bare breasts - then only in Paris possible, but my eyes were riveted on Fred.

That night I did not see the entire show, because the one glass was empty very soon, one more was too expensive.

I knew a little intimate gay-bar off the Faubourg St. Honore „Le petit Vendome". Three guys owned it and all spoke English and were very friendly. There was an empty seat at the bar. To my left sat a lady, obviously American, to my right a gent in a trench coat, ca. 50 I guessed. He talked to me first, „It started to rain and you without a coat", he shook his head and puffed on his stinking cigar. „I have seen you here before, no friends in town?" he said. „My coat is in my car, parked in front of the bar, and I do have friends", I lied.

„Oh, is that so! I was just about to offer to buy you a raincoat!" Maybe, if it has a fur lining", I said, grinning at him. „We can always start with the coat".

„No thank you", I said, „I've got one", turned my back to him and saw the lady in profile. She was smiling, studying her face in the mirror behind the bar.

„You seem to have been around, young man", she said, turned and face me. From her pillbox hat a little veil fell to the tip of her nose. She wore tons of make-up, her mouth painted fireman-red. Through her veil, black eyes looked at me with long glued-on lashes.

„It was not his first try", I said, „I with he would leave me alone".

In front of her stood a half empty glass of whisky, which she gulped down and ordered another one.

„Care for one?" she asked, but I declined politely.

„It's so boring to drink alone", she said, and motioned the barkeep to pay. He .pushed the bill towards her.

„That will be five whisky's Madame", he said.

She opened her tiny black purse. „Oh, Harry, I left my money in the hotel", she cried in horror and turning to me, „Could you help me out? I live in the „France + Choiseul" around the corner, we could go and get it".

„I am so sorry Madame, but I have not enough money with me", I said.

Harry interrupted, „That will be alright Mrs. Weiss until tomorrow".

She closed her purse, a short nod to me. „You are an angel, Harry", climbed off the bar stool and carefully balanced herself on her high heels to the exit.

With obvious relief Harry said to me „always the same thing, but she is loaded and good for the money".

„But why, Harry, does she hang around a gay bar?" I asked him.

„Loves gay young men, they are safe for her, loves their company, she is a very lonely lady", he said.

Suddenly I felt lonely, too, and paid.

„Tomorrow, tomorrow I shall not be lonely" I thought, and drove home.

It was the 14th July 1957. Paris went mad. My hangout was „Le Fiacre". The owner, Louis, had been very kind to me. He had watched me, a new face, and one night sat at my table and we talked in English.

„You know, you carry too much cash with you".

There are boys at the bar, their French is so perfect, you will think they are French but most of them are Germans like you are, be careful".

He was a slender fellow, very Latin looking, with a big moustache and large brown eyes. His gestures were strictly forties, in other words, he was very effeminate and always left a train of heavy perfume behind him.

Upstairs was a restaurant with a very mixed clientele, mostly artists and movie stars, who never bothered with the downstairs gay bar.

That night I sat by myself at a long banquette. Soon one was talking to their neighbours. The food was always excellent. Marcel, the waiter, flirted with me, which was not missed by the others, who found it amusing. After dinner, I went downstairs, had a few drinks and danced with Louis until Fred arrived. Everybody was in a fantastic mood. He had finally arrived, we embraced and kissed. On his face was still make-up, he had hurried to see me. We danced, we kissed. I was so happy to be with him. After an hour, I took him home to Neuilly and we made love all night until we fell asleep. Next morning he was gone, I checked my wallet, watch etc. It was all there. I heard the door open but pretended to be asleep. He carried in two big bags and the room filled with the smell of baguettes and croissants. He started to make coffee for us. „That one is ok", I thought, turned to the wall and dozed off to wait until he woke me up.

THE END

111